nancy rue
'NAMA BEACH HIGH
fault lines

Youth Specialties

www.youthspecialties.com

invert

ZONDERVAN™

WWW.ZONDERVAN.COM

'Nama Beach High Book 3: Fault Lines
Copyright © 2004 by Youth Specialties

Youth Specialties Books, 300 South Pierce Street, El Cajon, CA 92020, are published by Zondervan,
5300 Patterson Avenue SE, Grand Rapids, MI 49530

Library of Congress Cataloging-in-Publication Data

Rue, Nancy N.
  Fault lines / by Nancy Rue.
    p. cm. -- ('Nama Beach High ; bk. 3)
    Summary: With her jaw still wired shut from the last time she stood up
for what is right, Laura cannot help but get involved when local
"rednecks" harrass and intimidate a group of Jewish students newly
arrived from Israel.
    ISBN 0-310-25182-6 (softcover)
    [1. Toleration--Fiction. 2. Israelis--United States--Fiction. 3.
Jews--United States--Fiction. 4. High schools--Fiction. 5.
Schools--Fiction. 6. Christian life--Fiction.] I. Title.
  PZ7.R88515Fau 2004
  [Fic]--dc22

                                                                        2004008619

Unless otherwise indicated, all Scripture quotations are taken from the Holy Bible: New International
Version (North American Edition). Copyright © 1973, 1978, 1984 by International Bible Society. Used
by permission of Zondervan.

Web site addresses listed in this book were current at the time of publication. Please contact Youth
Specialties via e-mail (YS@YouthSpecialties.com) to report URLs that are no longer operational and
replacement URLs if available.

Editorial and art direction by Rick Marschall
Edited by Karyl Miller
Proofread by Laura Gross and Joanne Heim
Cover by Proxy
Interior by Sarah Jongsma
Printed in the United States of America

---

07 08 09 / DC / 10 9 8 7 6 5 4 3 2

chapter**one**

"**D**uffy," Celeste said to me in a whisper, "—could this possibly GET any more lame?"

At least, it fit Celeste's definition of a whisper, which meant everybody sitting within six feet of us heard it. That included our group—me (Laura Duffy), my girlfriends Stevie and Joy Beth, and Trent—plus four other kids, who had either dozed off or were so stupefied by boredom they couldn't even nod in agreement. One guy actually had drool oozing from the corner of his mouth.

"He's trying," Stevie whispered in my other ear. She nodded at the pastor perched on a stool in front of us—Pastor Ennis—who at the moment was clapping his hands into a clasp for about the five hundredth time. I was fairly certain his palms were going to slide off of each other the next time he did it. They had to be clammy by now. There were enough sweat beads sparkling on his high forehead to drown somebody. He was probably hoping at this point that it would be him.

"So, come on, folks, "he said. "I know there are some hot issues ya'll want to discuss."

"How about how to get ourselves out of here?" Celeste hissed to me.

"Somebody over here?" Pastor Ennis said. He looked so hopefully in our direction I knew he hadn't heard her exact words. But SOMEBODY had said SOMETHING, and he was grasping at it like the drowning man he was sure to be if he didn't wipe that forehead pretty soon.

Stevie raised her hand. He immediately grinned at her, which most people did the minute they laid eyes on her. If she hadn't been one of my best friends, I probably would have wanted to smack her for being so perfect. She had a smile that lit up her whole latte-colored, Latina-flavored face, including eyes that made you think of pure chocolate. You'd swear her smile even made her hair glow, although the highlights there came from a bottle and shone in big, loose, carefree curls. She raked a hand through them now

"Yes, ma'am!" Pastor said.

"I'm sure we all have issues," she said. She spread her smile over the eight teenagers in the room, actually waking up the kid with the drool problem. "But we don't know each other well enough to just start baring our souls."

She gave him another smile that clearly indicated it wasn't HIS fault that no one had spoken a word in the forty-five excruciating minutes since he'd called the "meeting" to order.

Pastor Ennis nodded seriously at her, his very-high forehead wrinkling into furrows all the way up to the cropped-short honey brown hair that predicted he'd be bald before he was forty. Thank heaven he didn't have a comb-over, or Celeste would have been beside herself. As it was, she was squirming like a little kid who had to go to the bathroom.

The pastor was still nodding. Drool Boy had gone back to sleep.

"So what you're saying is that we need to just—fellowship—get to know each other?"

"Right!" Stevie said. She made it sound like he'd just had a major break-through.

"So—then—" He glanced at his watch. "What do you say we break for refreshments and ya'll can mingle and get to know each other?"

Stevie opened her mouth to say something, but he had already disappeared through the doorway that led down the hall to the church kitchen.

Drool Boy opened his eyes and blinked. "Is it over?" he said.

"Did it ever start?" Celeste said.

Joy Beth grunted, and then exchanged glances with Trent. I knew what the grunt meant—it was Joy-Beth-ese for "You got that right." But the look with Trent, that I hadn't figured out yet. They'd only been an item for about a month, and I knew they were totally into each other

because she grunted at him more than she ever did at anybody else, and
he actually spoke whole paragraphs to her which were NOT about
nuclear physics or differential calculus.

Pastor Ennis reappeared carrying a cooler, and his cute pixie-haired
wife followed with seven Domino's Pizza boxes. Nine people couldn't have
eaten that much sausage and pepperoni if we'd been starved on a desert
island. Make that eight people. Drool Boy had wandered out the door.

"Ya'll eat up and mingle and break the ice," Reverend Ennis said.
"We're going to give you some space."

"I hope he takes a Valium," Celeste said, her husky voice, thicker
than usual with Brooklynese. "Dude's a nervous wreck."

"I don't think he's ever tried to start a youth group before," Stevie said.

Joy Beth grunted. "What was your first clue?"

"You better eat some of that pizza," I said.

I definitely couldn't eat any. I still had my jaw wired shut from having
it broken a month before. Nothing went into my mouth unless it entered
through a plastic syringe that looked like it was designed for Big Bird's
vaccinations. I could talk, teeth clenched together, but between the wires
and the orthodontia I was already equipped with, I was slowed down in
the verbal department. Celeste had gotten pretty accustomed to talking
FOR me.

I put one hand on Celeste's back and one on Stevie's, and we went to
the table where the three remaining kids pretty much had the extra-large
"All the Meats" devoured. I was pretty sure they had stuffed their mouths
so they wouldn't have to talk. Laura the Responsible One kicked in. After
all, I was the only one who knew their names because I was the one who
went to church there at Cove Community. Celeste went with me
sometimes. I had dragged Stevie and Joy Beth and Trent to this meeting
with a promise of coffee at Books-A-Million—my treat—when it was over.
If it ever WAS over.

I tapped each of my friends with a finger.

"Celeste Mancini, Joy Beth Barnes, Trent Newell, Stevie Martinez—
meet Alex, Genevieve, and Vanessa." I shrugged, rather ungracefully, and
added, "Sorry I don't know your last names."

"It's not like there's going to be a test," Stevie said. She offered her
hand to shake Vanessa's and gave her the smile.

Alex stuck his paw out and lifted his eyelids above half mast for the
first time the whole evening. "How long do we have to stay without it
looking like we're ditching him?" he said to her.

"How long can you stand it?" Celeste said.

Alex then focused in on Celeste—blonde hair draping down from her white visor, freckles dancing across a sunburned nose that refused to be anything but absolutely real—and then looked back at Stevie as if he couldn't decide which one to hit on first. I resisted the urge to roll my eyes. Feeling like the over-lookable sidekick was the downside of having drop-dead gorgeous friends—even when I wasn't talking like I had lockjaw. I was pretty white-bread, built like a Missouri bean pole, with hair that wasn't completely red or completely brown, and generic brown eyes. My only really distinguishing feature was the ruddy color of my Midwestern corn-fed cheeks, which betrayed my every emotion with a simple change of hue.

"I've already stood it longer than I can," Alex was saying.

"We wouldn't let him split," Genevieve said. "Our dad's the Mac Daddy at this church. If he found out, we'd have to mow the church lawn or something."

"I'd rather do that," Joy Beth said.

She would. Anything requiring physical activity appealed to Joy Beth. Swimming was her big thing, though only recently had the docs let her start practicing with the team again because her diabetes was finally under control. She'd be on the John Deere right now if it meant getting out of standing around trying to think of something to say. She looked up at big ol' bad-hair-day Trent through her panels of lanky, not-quite-blonde hair, and he blinked down at her, as usual, as if his contacts were malfunctioning.

"We're tryin' to think of some heinous punishment for Duffy," Celeste said, nudging me. "She dragged ALL of us here."

Stevie glanced over her shoulder at the Ennises, who were sitting in a far corner of the room trying not to look like they were watching us, and leaned in. "At least he tried."

"Now he can check it off his to-do list," Alex said. "I personally don't need a youth group. I've got my own friends—I come to church—I obey the Ten Commandments—I'm good to go."

Vanessa looked up at him with a cocked eyebrow. "ALL of them?"

"Let me guess which ones you're missing," Celeste said.

Laura the Responsible One said, "Could we not go there? We need to come up with some 'hot topics' for Pastor."

"That's what I'm doing." Celeste wiggled her sandy eyebrows at Alex. "Whatever commandments he's not obeying are probably some pretty hot topics."

"There's a really good reason why I don't 'obey' them," Alex said. He gave a square grin. "Because I don't WANT to. Look, if you guys decide to plan a 'youth group' beach party, I'm there. Otherwise, forget it."

"I think we've stayed long enough," Vanessa said. "I have SO much homework to do."

"You think he'd mind if we took some of this with us?" Alex said.

Trent picked up two pizza boxes and handed them to him.

"Could they have BEEN any more rude?" Stevie said as Alex and his two sisters headed for the door, a double cheese with pepperoni in their possession, without a word to the Ennisses.

"I can't look," I said. I poked Celeste. "Does Pastor look totally humiliated?"

"He looks like—'THAT didn't go well'," Stevie said.

"It didn't," Joy Beth said.

"So here we are—'getting to know each other'," I said. "Anybody ready to bare your soul?"

"That's all we do!" Stevie said. "My emotions are naked when I'm with y'all."

"I'm so glad you didn't say that in front of Mr. 'Don't-You-Think-I'm-Sexy'," Celeste said, nodding in Alex's wake. "He would have jumped you right here."

"That's an image I can live without," Stevie said.

"So what are we going to do?" I said. "I don't want to hurt Pastor Ennis's feelings. He did try. And youth groups CAN be a blast. I used to go to one when I first moved here...."

"Here they come," Joy Beth muttered. She turned her face to Trent's chest. He selected his fifth piece of pizza and gave it his full attention.

Stevie directed the smile at the Ennisses, while Celeste put her lips to my ear. "Are you thinkin' about that group you used to go to with Richard?" she whispered.

"Yeah," I said.

"Are you thinkin' about Richard?"

"No!"

"Liar. Your first date with him was at a youth group beach party."

"Okay, yeah. So?"

I actually hadn't allowed myself to think about Richard in months. Even now, as memory pulled into view of his shiny hair tousled over his forehead as he pulled me up the sand dunes at St. Andrew's Bay State Park, smiling a shiny smile full of more braces than I had, looking down at me with his head cocked in a way that made me feel like nothing else could, I didn't spend more than a few seconds looking at it. After all, there was Owen now...

Besides, thinking about Richard did strange things to the color of my cheeks. They either turned scarlet with embarrassment, or purple with hidden anger. It was safer just not to go there.

Pastor Ennis stepped in beside me and shoved his hands into his pockets. I noticed that at some point he had wiped the perspiration off his face. Probably that cute little wife had taken care of that.

He looked down at me from six-foot-two. "How did ya'll think it went?"

Nobody spoke. Even Stevie was waiting for me to be the one to verbalize the poor guy's humiliation.

Hello, God? I thought. *A little help here?*

There was no whisper, no gentle tug, which meant I probably didn't need any help. What was there to say except the truth? Besides, Celeste looked like she was about to blurt something out, so I said quickly, "We really appreciate you trying to get a group together. It's hard, though, to just—start talking."

Pastor Ennis nodded, his face solemn. "Maybe I should have started with the pizza."

"Or an ice-breaker," Stevie said.

"Something for people to do so they don't even know you're trying to get them to make nice," Celeste said.

I gave her sleeve a tug. She gave me the big blue-eyed "What? What'd I say?" look. She was absolutely my best friend in the world, but she had the tact of a large semi tractor-trailer rig. Must be because she was from New York.

"Thanks for being honest," Pastor Ennis said. "You want to take some of this pizza home? I was expecting a bigger turn-out."

I felt a pang for him. He was looking pretty vulnerable.

Trent took him up on the pizza offer, and we all thanked him and Mrs. Ennis, who was probably going to have to talk her husband out of a major funk when they got home. We couldn't pile into Stevie's Ford Expedition fast enough.

Actually, it wasn't Stevie's—it was her dad's. He let her use it, though, every time the five of us went someplace together. Celeste and I each drove an old Mercedes fixed up by her father, neither of which was big enough for Trent alone, much less the rest of us. Trent wasn't a jock like Joy Beth, but he was big and hulky and had legs the size of thirty-year-old tree trunks. He himself didn't have a driver's license. Joy Beth did, but their family had Daddy's pick-up truck and Mama's nine-passenger van for the toting of the seven Barnes offspring. Neither of those vehicles was ever available for Joy Beth's recreation.

"You SO owe us, Duffy," Celeste said as Stevie pulled the Expedition into the Books-A-Million parking lot. "I'm ordering a double mocha."

"Would you quit your whinin'?" I said. "You would think I put you in front of a firing squad."

Books-A-Million wasn't crowded, not the way it was on Friday and Saturday nights when half the high school kids in Panama Beach crammed in there to hang out. There was only one other group of students in the coffee shop area that night, sitting on the couch and soft chairs by the window. As we dropped our stuff off at our usual table and went for the counter, Stevie put her lips close to my ear.

"It's that new girl in second period," she murmured. "Shouldn't we say hi to her?"

"Just don't expect her to say hi back," Celeste said, as under-her-breath as she could manage. "She's in my P.E. class. I tried to talk to her—y'know—I'm from New York, I heard she's from New York, that kinda thing." Her face went blank. "It was like talkin' to a tree. Double mocha," she said to the girl behind the counter. "With extra whipped cream."

"Are they all from New York?" Stevie said. She tapped CAPPUCINO on the menu with her fingernail and smiled at the counter girl. "They all came at the same time, and they all look kind of alike—they have to be from the same family."

Trent looked at Joy Beth. "Wanna share an Italian soda?"

"Too cute!" Celeste said to Stevie and me behind her hand.

I didn't order anything. I didn't usually whip the Big Bird syringe out in public places, except at school where everybody had pretty much seen it—although they still stared. Only a few more weeks and the doctor would clip the wires. If my jaw was completely healed, the first thing I was going to do was sing—and sing—and sing. It had been the worst part of not being able to open my mouth. I had a new Jami Smith CD I played constantly in my car, and all I wanted to do was belt out those songs.

And then I was going to go to Burger King and order a Double Whopper with Cheese. I would be picking pieces of that out of my braces for days, but that was okay, because very soon after that, those babies were coming off too.

While the gang waited for their orders, I took a few curious peeks at the group by the window. I could have probably all-out gaped at them, because they appeared to be deep in serious conversation. They probably hadn't even noticed that we'd come in. That had pretty much been my experience with the one girl in the group that I'd had any contact with.

What do they call her? I thought. *Hadassah?*

It wasn't your typical Florida Panhandle name. "Joy Beth" was more what you heard where we lived.

When we finally got organized around the table, Trent gave Joy Beth first drag on the soda and said, "Israel."

Celeste gazed around at the ceiling.

"What about Israel, Trentsky?" I said.

He nodded only slightly toward the other group. "They moved here from New York, but originally they're from Israel."

"Like, born there?" Celeste said.

"Yeah. That one guy's in physics with me."

"Which one?" Stevie said.

"Dark-haired kid."

Celeste blinked. "They ALL have dark hair, Trent."

"The one in the black shirt. Name's Uri."

"Is he friendly?" Stevie said.

He shrugged. "He seems like he's hacked off all the time."

Celeste was nodding. Her usually impish blue eyes were suddenly serious.

"What?" I said to her.

"You can't really blame him—or the chick—Hosanna or whatever her name is."

"Hadassah," Stevie and I said together.

The group by the window stirred, and both Stevie and I broke into automatic smiles and waved. Hadassah nodded and went back to their conversation.

"You can't blame 'em," Celeste said again. "They've been getting hassled ever since they got here."

"By who?" I said. "Not Gigi and them?"

"Are you kidding?" Stevie said. "Gigi and Wendy are doing back flips to stay out of trouble. You know the judge gave them probation, right?"

We gave a simultaneous nod. She didn't have to mention their male counterparts, who were actually in a juvenile detention facility after what they'd pulled. My broken jaw was only part of it.

"Then who's hassling them?" I said.

"Rednecks," Joy Beth said.

I choked back a laugh. Joy Beth was really the only one of us who could say that, because she considered herself to be one. Personally, I didn't care WHAT she was. I loved her like a sister.

"Militant rednecks," Trent put in. "NRA—KKK—"

Celeste's eyes popped. "What—you're talking Ruby Ridge?"

"No," Stevie said. "I think they're just wanna-be's. But they will NOT leave those poor kids alone."

"That's probably what they're talking about over there," Celeste said.

"What's the deal, though?" I said. "What have the—'rednecks'—got against them?"

Joy Beth drew her pale gray eyes together into a scowl and folded the arms that put most high school wrestlers to shame. "They're just ignorant. Anybody who's a foreigner they think oughta be run outa town."

"Oh," Stevie said. "So the fact that they're from Israel makes it even worse."

"How come?" I said.

"That's what I love about you, Laura, you're so innocent," she said.

"Nine-eleven, Duffy," Celeste said. "Anybody who's from someplace like Iraq or somethin', people think they're terrorists."

I gaped openly at the seven Israeli kids who were dipping biscotti into their mugs. They all had straight black hair, dark eyes, rich-olive skin. They all looked serious, in a way that went deeper than our momentary lapses into somber subjects. And two of them—Hadassah and Uri—seemed to have something smoldering just beneath the surface. While the others looked wary, those two looked—what was it? It wasn't anger. Their primary emotion wasn't something that was going to pop open in a fit and then burn away. This was something that lived in them. I got the feeling it had been living there for a long time.

"So, is there, like, some reason to think they ARE terrorists?" Celeste was saying. "I'm just asking."

Trent shrugged. "Uri doesn't say the pledge to the flag."

"Neither do half the losers in the school," Celeste said. "Doesn't mean they're gonna strap on a suicide bomb."

"Besides," Stevie said, "they're not Muslims—not that THAT automatically makes them terrorists either. They're Jews."

Celeste pulled her neck up, ET style. "Then why are we even having this conversation? I grew UP with Jewish kids in New York. They gave me

Chanukkah presents, for Pete's sake. None of 'em would even step on a cockroach. I beat one kid up one time and he didn't even hit me back."

"You beat someone UP?" Stevie said. "Why?"

"Because he said my mother was a drug addict," Celeste said calmly. "She WAS, but I didn't like hearin' it from other kids, you know what I'm sayin'?"

I pulled my eyes reluctantly away from the Jewish family.

"What's going on, Duffy?" Celeste said. "I know that look."

"I just want to know more about them," I said. "Just a feeling."

Stevie chuckled. "All we have to do is ask K.J. in group tomorrow. She probably knows their whole family history by now."

There was a scraping of chairs from across the room. The group was getting up and moving toward the door.

"See you guys," Celeste called to them.

Only Hadassah looked over her shoulder. She gave a nod you would have had to replay in slow motion to make sure it was really a nod and followed her family out the door.

"I'm getting another soda," Trent said, and headed for the counter.

"Okay," Celeste said to us girls. "Duffy, I wanna know what's going on with Owen. Does he email you, like, everyday—"

But she was suddenly drowned out by the roar of an engine being revved up just outside the door. Tires squealed, and I jolted from my seat in time to see a too-high pick-up truck peal out of a parking place—and then remain still, its engine winding out as the driver obviously pumped the accelerator.

From the parking space next to the one the truck had just vacated, a Lincoln Navigator, filled with the Israeli students, pulled out at a sedate pace and left the lot. The passenger in the truck hauled his upper body out the window. And then he hurled a bottle after it.

chaptertwo

We were at the window in three collective strides, along with Counter Girl and the manager. But even before we got there, the over-sized tires of the truck had squealed it off in the opposite direction. A motorcycle shot out behind it. The shards of the bottle lay glittering in the lights of the parking lot, and the Lincoln SUV was long gone.

"Rednecks," the manager muttered under his breath. He marched toward bookstore check-out and smacked his palm on the counter. "Get somebody from the back to clean that up," he said, and then pulled the pencil from behind his ear and returned to his computer print-out.

"Hey," Celeste called to him. "Aren't you callin' the cops?"

He looked at her as if she wanted him to report a UFO. "What am I gon' tell 'em? You get a license plate number?"

"No," Stevie said. "But we can describe the truck. It looked like it was sanded down –"

"Primed," Celeste said.

"Big tires," I said.

He looked at me with the most interest he'd shown in anything so far. He was probably the only person in Panama Beach who hadn't seen the chick in the wires yet.

"That about describes every other vehicle between here and Apalachicola, now don't it?" he said. He turned back to the counter.

"You get somebody to clean that up? All I need is some guy suing me because he blows a tire."

"What about those poor kids they threw the bottle at?" Stevie said.

Mr. Manager Man gave us one last look. "What kids?" he said.

"Stupid redneck," Joy Beth mumbled.

That about summed it up.

On the way to my house to drop me off, Stevie and the rest of them went over the thing, coming to the conclusion that the people in the truck were probably the "Redneck Militia," just waiting out there to put the fear into the Israeli kids. I didn't say much. All I could think about was what simmered beneath the deep-olive skins of Hadassah and Uri. As I closed my eyes, I could see it filtering from their pores like steam, but I had no idea what it meant.

Stevie pulled the Expedition into the driveway of the only pink stucco house in the Cove. Mine. At least it wasn't quite as hideous as it had been when we'd moved into it six months before, only because my father spent almost every hour he wasn't working for T-Mobile making it something the Duffys "could be proud to call their home."

"You okay, Duff'?" Stevie said as I opened the door.

"Yeah," I said.

"You are such a liar," Celeste said. "It's smeared all over your face. That really got to you."

"Yeah," I said again. "I just think we have to pray for them—those Israeli kids."

"Done," Stevie said.

Joy Beth grunted, Trent nodded, and Celeste pulled her torso out through the window to plant a big ol' kiss on my cheek. I loved those people.

Even though it was only nine o'clock, the house was dark except for the light over the kitchen sink. I could smell the oatmeal before I even got there. Dad was just pouring it into the blender, Big Bird's syringe at the ready.

"Hey," I said.

"Hey, Baby Girl. Sit down. Take a load off." He looked at me and grimaced. "Load? More like a tenth of a load. I'll be glad when those wires come off and we can get some meat on your bones." He pushed the button on the blender.

All of that would seem like a normal exchange between a father and a daughter, especially with a dad who had a hard time just saying "I love you." But for MY father and ME, it was a miracle that had started happening almost every night since my jaw got broken. Mom got Bonnie to bed—no small feat—and then shortly thereafter fell in herself—and Dad fixed cereal for the two of us. Then we sat at the kitchen table and talked about whatever came up, at times bordering on wanting to smack each other, but duking it out verbally instead.

Six months before—when I was so ticked off at him, among other things for moving me away from my Missouri home and all I'd ever known—or even TWO months before—when he had being the I-Know-All father down to an art form—I would have said these nightly meetings would be impossible, if not downright nauseating. But now, I actually looked forward to them.

Dad set the syringe with its little rubber tube next to the bowl of oatmeal in front of me. It was on a green and white checked placemat, of course—my mother's contribution. She'd recently done the kitchen in apples, but Dad had said if she got apple placemats he knew he was going to turn INTO a Winesap.

"I put real butter and two sugars in that," Dad said now, "and I want you to eat it all."

"I don't have a problem with that," I said. "I watched people scarf down pizza and whipped cream all night. I'm starving."

"How was the youth group thing?"

I rolled my eyes.

"Pretty bad, huh?"

"Pastor Ennis tried, but he needs help."

"And you volunteered, of course."

I shook my head as I pushed a mouthful of oatmeal behind my back teeth.

"I'm surprised," Dad said, lifting his red-brown-like-mine eyebrows. Actually his, like his hair, were peppered with gray. I'd probably been responsible for most of that just since we'd moved to Florida, as well as the weight loss that made him look tall and drawn. "Too bad it can't be like that other outfit you were going to for a while."

"Outfit?" I said.

"Yeah—with that Richard character. Whatever happened to him?"

There was a time when I could have filled my mouth with mush and not said anything and he would have let it go, but anymore, he was all over everything like Dr. Phil. Besides—I hadn't thought about Richard in months, and now twice in one night somebody was bringing it up. That probably meant I ought to at least look at it.

"I was too pushy," I said. "I got too serious."

"Define serious."

I sighed. Still didn't work. He just kept looking at me as he chewed.

"I wanted this big commitment thing," I said. "And that scared him off."

He toyed with his Corn Flakes with the tip of his spoon. "You have a 'big commitment thing' with Owen?"

"No. That would be kind of pointless with him living all the way across the state now."

"Probably wise, although your mother and I had a long-distance relationship in college. Of course, we were older."

I was staring. This was definitely a quantum leap in the father-daughter thing—him divulging a single detail about my mother's and his "relationship."

I pretended not to be flabbergasted and said, ultra-casually, "How did you two keep it going?"

"I told her if she so much as looked at another guy, I'd come to Wesleyan and punch his lights out."

I looked up in time to see the tiny crinkles appearing around his eyes. "You so did not!"

"Nah," he said. "I have a life-sized picture of me doing that."

Me, too. Dad was about as scary-looking as Mister Rogers. "To tell you the truth," he said, "I don't know how we did it. Just fumbled through, I guess."

I tried to erase the instant image of him and my mom "fumbling" and gave an understanding nod behind which I had no clue at all.

"When Owen left, we said we were just friends," I said. "Owen says I should date other people and have a good time. I know it doesn't bother you that I'm not going out with him any more. You never really liked him."

"I never said that!" Dad actually looked wounded. "He's a nice kid—he was good to you. I just couldn't get into the earring and the dyed hair."

"Well, anyway, I can't imagine myself going out with anybody else right now. Most boys are so immature."

"You sure go through them."

I stared. "Dad—Owen's only the second guy I've ever even liked, and I'm almost seventeen!"

"What about that one fella that risked his neck for you and Trent? He just up and disappeared."

He was talking about the guy that my friends always referred to as Ponytail Boy. He'd been there for us on more than one occasion, but none of us really knew him, and he hadn't been around in the last month. He was a whole other thing. It was time for a topic change.

"So—what do you know about Jews from Israel?" I said.

He stopped scraping the bottom of his bowl. "Where in the world did that come from?"

I told him about what happened at Books-A-Million. He narrowed his brown eyes at me. "Laura—I know the kind of thing that goes on in your head, and I respect that. But please—let the authorities handle any trouble that comes up, all right?" He scraped back his chair. "I'm not saying 'don't care', because I know you can't help it. But you haven't even healed from the last battle yet."

Dad picked up my bowl and took them both to the sink. When he turned back around to face me, his crinkles had softened into tiny, puffy folds. "I'm proud of you, Baby Girl," he said. "Just—no more trips to the emergency room, okay?"

"Deal," I said.

Dad went into the family room to read, and he was snoring in his green leather recliner within ten minutes. I tiptoed to his desk, a few feet away, and sat down at the computer. The announcement, "You've got mail!" was like the "Hallelujah Chorus" to my ears. There was a message from Owen.

I knew there was no point in I.M.ing him because they were an hour ahead of us in Jacksonville and he'd be zonked out by now. He got up at 4:00 a.m. to work at UPS until his classes started at JU at 9:00. I ate up every word of his emails, even though he always kept them "friendly".

Hey, Girlfriend—

What's up? Same old thing here. My mother is "responding to treatment" at the clinic. That's the way they talk, those doctors. Her BDI has already gone from 50 down to 37 which basically means I don't have to worry that I'm going to find her on the bathroom floor with an empty bottle of barbiturates in her hand.

I dyed my hair blonde, just to see what it would look like. Soon as I find somebody with a digital camera, I'll email you a picture. I'm not meeting many people I could hit up for a camera, actually. I work, go to class, study, go back to work—email you. As soon as that scholarship kicks in, I'm getting a cell phone and then I'll be able to call you. I miss your voice—even squeezing out through those wires.

Owen

I rested my forehead against the screen. What I wouldn't give to hear Owen's voice—the voice that made me feel like I was as beautiful and fun as Stevie or Celeste. Everything made sense when I could talk to Owen.

* * *

I had a doctor's appointment the next morning—Dr. McKinley said I was right on schedule for getting my wires clipped in a few weeks—so I didn't get to school until second period. I went to my locker, and for a second or two, I looked longingly into it. A little note from my "Secret Admirer" would be a nice touch about now—just a few lines written on parchment paper to let me know he hadn't disappeared completely. But then, he usually only left his cryptic little clues when I was really confused or headed down the wrong track. Maybe, I decided, no note meant I was okay, in spite of a certain funkiness that was creeping up on me.

I walked into history class in the middle of Mr. Beecher setting up the class for a current events "discussion." It was a MAPPS course (which meant advanced placement and accelerated and every other superlative you could think of), but although most of the kids in there could ace any test Mr. Beecher could produce, we weren't that good at keeping up with what was going on around the globe. It wasn't that none of us cared about the world—but when you were working like a slave to keep your GPA up and prep for the SAT and ACT, plus be involved in some activities so you didn't look like a complete geek on your college applications, who the Sam Hill had time to tune into CNN and read the *New York Times*?

As I slipped into my desk next to Stevie's, I could sense that Mr. Beecher was on a mission. He had a line between his eyebrows deep as a trench, which usually translated as I am about to make you THINK.

"You've read the article I assigned," he said.

I'd managed to get that done before I'd dozed off the night before. "U.S. Dilemma: Facing Reality." It was about Iraq mostly.

"Now," Mr. Beecher said, "I have a question that I want you to think about. THINK about, not vomit back to me what you've read."

"That is just gross," muttered the girl behind us.

"I want you each to jot down some notes for yourself—I will give you five minutes. Then I want you in groups of three to share your reactions. And then I want you back as a whole tomorrow where I had better hear some THOUGHTS, some EDUCATED OPINIONS being volunteered—or I will start asking people point blank and deducting points for having absolutely no clue. Am I clear?"

THAT definitely struck fear into some hearts. There were people in that class who would have sold their mothers into slavery if it meant raising their class standing. I used to be one of them, but I no longer lived for the day when I would get a scholarship to an Ivy League School. I still did the absolute best I could. But I focused more on music, my friends, and God. Not necessarily in that order. I was more and more into a relationship with God all the time—He just wouldn't leave me alone.

As Mr. Beecher turned to write the question on the board, Stevie leaned into me. "Let's get Hadassah in our group," she whispered. "You ask her. I don't think she likes me."

"I don't think she likes anybody," I whispered back. But I swiveled around and stretched across the aisle to put my hand on the edge of Hadassah's desktop one seat back. She had both eyebrows raised over the assigned article, two thick accents on her mocha-colored forehead.

"Will you work with Stevie and me?" I whispered to her.

She removed her glasses—a very classy-looking pair of gold wire rims —and gave me a look that pierced clear back to my medulla oblongata. "It is not going to mean instant points," she said. "I am Israeli, not Iraqi."

"I know!" I said.

I was sure I sounded like Bonnie insisting that she knew how to operate the microwave by herself, thank you very much. Hadassah must have had some sense of that, because she put her glasses back on, returned to the article, and said, "Fine."

"That went well," I whispered to Stevie.

I went through the piece once again and squinted up at Mr. Beecher's question.

HAS U.S. OCCUPATION OF IRAQ INCREASED GLOBAL TERRORISM OR MADE IT MORE EASY TO DEFEAT?

How the heck am I supposed to know what generals and people with PhDs. can't even figure out? I thought. *If I did, the freakin' United Nations would hire me!*

But I did feel a little pulled toward getting to know Hadassah. If I weren't being tugged by the silky rope that seemed to connect God and me, I wouldn't have gone there. Hadassah was so coldly aloof, she made me want to say, "I'm sorry" when I hadn't even done anything to her.

"Into your groups," Mr. Beecher said.

We took three abandoned desks near the door—everybody else had shoved their furniture toward the back of the room, as if Mr. Beecher

WEREN'T going to be policing the area like the Gestapo—and I drew a line under the few paltry thoughts I'd written down, pen poised.

"So what is it you want me to do?" Hadassah said. "Dictate while you take notes and you—" she nodded at Stevie—"present the information to the class?"

Stevie leaned across the desks and leveled her eyes at Hadassah. "We want to work with you because we know you're serious about things like this. Everybody else is going to spend half the time talking about how much they don't CARE what happens in Iraq."

"Or anyplace else, for that matter," I said. "Can you understand me okay? I know it's hard with the wires. Everybody else is used to it by now, but—"

"I am understanding your meaning," Hadassah said. "So, DO you care what happens in the Middle East?"

"I care about the people over there," I said. "I just don't know enough to say who's right and who's wrong."

Hadassah was peering at me through her glasses with her eyes narrowed. I had to resist the urge to look up and see if there was a naked light bulb hanging over us. Didn't I get one phone call?

"At least you recognize that there IS a problem, which is more than I can say for any of the other students I have met in this school."

She spoke very smoothly, as if English, correct English, were her native language. It reminded me of her hair: like thick, dark silk. I bet she was ruining the curve on Mrs. Wren's grammar tests in the fourth period section.

"But I cannot blame any of you, really," she went on.

"Why not?" Stevie said. "We're ignorant!"

"Only because you CAN be. You have never lived in the midst of constant bombings and shootings and death and fear. We did not have a choice—we had to think of these things, just to remain alive."

I didn't know whose eyes were opening wider, Stevie's or mine.

"Is that why you left Israel?" Stevie said.

That steam of something passionate was seeping from Hadassah again. "My family came to this country to escape the violence—yes."

She's not exactly doing cartwheels about that, I thought. I had a vague vision of her parents dragging her kicking and screaming onto a plane in Tel-Aviv.

"As for American teenagers—" Hadassah wrote the whole lot of us off with a shrug of her thin, elegant shoulders. "I do not see that you live with enough passion to stand up for anything more important than who wins a football game."

Stevie leaned forward, eyes locked into Hadassah's. "Maybe that's because we can," she said.

"That is why my father brought us here," Hadassah said. "So that we, too, can grow up thinking of nothing but such things."

"But you don't want to be here."

"There is a reason why God made me a Jew in Israel. I do not believe it was so that I could run away."

"That child is scary," Stevie said to me after class.

"We have to find out what K.J. knows," I said.

chapterthree

We had our Thursday group meeting in Mrs. Isaacsen's office during activity period that day, and Stevie and I were the first ones there so we could get to K.J. and pump her for information before the session started.

I didn't think it would be hard. Although K.J. was only a freshman, she seemed to know everyone in the school. She made it her business to know, as if she always wanted to ferret out which causes to go up against the administration on and how she could protect herself in the process. Not only was her father the Chief of Police for Panama Beach—daunting enough in itself—but if she got into any trouble at ALL in school, she'd be taken out of the production of *The Crucible* that was now in rehearsal.

She had a pretty big role as Mary Warren, and it was her LIFE at that point. But even if she wasn't going to get "involved" with the Israeli students, she'd be sure to know most of the details of their lives by now. After all, they'd been there a whole two weeks.

My precious Mrs. Isaacsen—the most amazing counselor in the galaxy—was bustling around her office, setting up the circle of chairs for the six of us girls and her. I gave her the usual hug and got a whiff of her Chantilly powder and morning cup of coffee. She and I were actually "tea junkies," as she put it, but the scent of that one cup of Columbian blend at the start of the day seemed to linger with her always. Breathing it in was like eating comfort food.

She gave me a squeeze back, her slightly thick-around-the-waist body warm and her short, crispy, black-and-gray hair brushing against my cheek. There was a crinkly-eyed smile for me as we pulled apart and she perched the half-glasses-on-a-chain on the end of her nose to look at me more closely.

"You're on a mission, Laura," she said, dark eyes dancing.

"Is K.J. here yet?" Stevie said. "We want to grill her."

Mrs. I. chuckled. "At least you're honest. I'm surprised Celeste isn't in on this, whatever it is."

"She is," Stevie said. She flashed the smile, and Mrs. I. grinned back. Stevie had only been in our group for a month, but it was obvious Mrs. Isaacsen loved her as much as she did me and Celeste and K.J. and Joy Beth and Michelle. I loved them all, too, although my affection for Michelle was a little more rational than heartfelt. Michelle didn't let you in like the other girls in the group did.

The door opened and K.J. came in, with Celeste on her heels. She was evidently in mid-interrogation, but from the look on K.J.'s face, she wasn't getting anywhere. Stevie and I exchanged puzzled glances.

K.J. was wearing a scowl between her wide-set, oblong brown eyes, and she was tossing the light chin-length hair back from her face like the strands—and Celeste—were mosquitoes that were bothering the heck out of her. The "you want a piece of me?" look was clearly etched in her expression.

It wasn't as if we'd never seen that look before, but it was usually reserved for her father, any member of the faculty and staff except Mrs. Isaacsen and Mr. Howitch, the music/drama teacher, and any of us who wouldn't answer HER personal questions. For her to look exasperated when being asked to share information she prided herself on getting was unusual to say the least.

K.J. stopped in front of one of the chairs and dropped her backpack soundly on the floor. Giving her leopard stretch top a yank to cover her belly button, and the denim jacket a tug to conceal the spaghetti straps, she turned on Celeste.

"If I tell you what I know, will you leave me alone?" she said through gritted teeth.

"Absolutely," Celeste said. She slid into the chair next to K.J.'s and looked up at Mrs. I. "Do we have time?"

"The bell hasn't rung yet," Mrs. I. said. "And then you know after that the rules go into effect."

"Gotcha." Celeste whipped back to K.J. Since she herself was decked out Asian-style, in an embroidered silk jacket with a mandarin collar and chopsticks in the bun on top of her head, the two of them were a study in fashion contrasts. When Joy Beth came in, she didn't even give it a second glance. We were all used to K.J. seeing how much she could get away with and Celeste trying on a new look everyday.

"So dish," Celeste said.

K.J. folded her arms and spoke in a monotone. "This whole huge family moved down here from New York. Last name's Dayan. It's like three brothers and their wives and kids. The one brother is like the head of the whole clan and he decided he could do whatever it is he does better down here than he could in New York City."

"So we know he's not in the bagel business," Celeste said.

"You want to hear this or not?" K.J. said.

Her voice bristled like a dog brush. Stevie and Celeste raised eyebrows at each other. I felt squirmy.

"Go for it," Celeste said.

"The main brother has three kids here at 'Nama—Hadassah, Uri, and Nava. The other two brothers have seven more kids—so there's ten going here. Hadassah and Uri are like the leaders of the kids, and their little sister is like the runt of the whole litter and everybody protects her, especially Uri. They're Jewish—they're originally from Israel—they were only in New York a month and a half before they moved here."

"And they speak English that well?" I said. "Hadassah uses better grammar than all of us put together."

"Their mother's Israeli, but she went to school in New York so she always talked English to them since they were babies."

Celeste snorted. "That don't mean it was good English. You oughta hear some of my relatives talk."

"Your relatives?" K.J. said

The bell rang, and K.J. pulled her knees up to her chest and closed into herself. If she'd made that remark to Celeste after the bell, Mrs. I. would have been all over her. We had strict rules in group: no negative remarks about people, no "fixing," and every response had to be in the form of a question. K.J.'s slap at Celeste was technically a question, but Mrs. Isaacsen wouldn't have let it go.

Besides that, it surprised me. When we'd first started meeting as a group back in October, K.J. had snarled like that all the time, like she was building a barbed wire fence around herself. But gradually she'd stopped doing that, especially since she'd gotten the role in *The Crucible*. It seemed like with her acting dream starting to come true, she didn't have to stomp on everybody else's dreams anymore.

Something is way wrong, I thought. *And if she keeps up that attitude, Mr. Howitch won't keep her in the play.*

'Nama Beach High had the top music/drama department on the whole Panhandle, if not beyond. People practically killed to get into his productions, so he didn't have to put up with what he called "Rude Tudes." The fact that he had changed his mind from doing "The Glass Menagerie," which only had four roles, to "The Crucible," which had about a jillion, so that he could include people like K.J. made his cast and crew check their Tudes at the theater door.

"All right, ladies," Mrs. I. said. "Let's get started."

Even though that day Mrs. I. asked us to reassess where we now felt powerful and where we still considered ourselves powerless, K.J. stayed quiet and sullen the whole session. When the bell rang, Mrs. I. asked her to stay behind. Michelle took off, as always, as if she were headed for a board meeting. The rest of us joined Trent at our usual table out in the courtyard and broke out our brown bags. It was late-April Florida-warm, and the place was more filled-up than usual with kids in shorts and tank tops parking in the sunny places to start on their tans.

I peeked into my Tupperware container at the cottage cheese concoction my mother had whipped up in the blender for Big Bird's syringe.

Celeste wrinkled her nose. "Lovely," she said.

"It's better than Ensure," I said.

Stevie nudged me from across the table with her knee, a turkey wrap suspended between her insulated lunch bag and her mouth.

"There's Hadassah," she said.

I watched the silken mane of hair trail after the Jewish girl as she strode across the courtyard toward three round tables filled with what had to be the clan K.J. had begrudgingly described to us.

"Should we ask her to sit with us?" I said.

Celeste grunted. "You mean Miss Congeniality?"

"If she's like her brother," Trent said, "do ya'll mind if I digest my food first?" He took an impressive bite out of a thick ham sandwich with his very-small-for-a-guy-that-big mouth.

"She probably won't come," I said. "But I think we should at least ask—"

I was cut off by a raucous, grating voice that said: "Hey, Hussein— whatta you think yer doin'?"

I snapped my head around so hard I could hear my neck bones crackling. It was amazing I could hear anything except the cigarette-deep voice that was blasting into the face of Hadassah's brother, Uri. He was in an awkward half-sit, his lunch bag still several inches from the table top as a scrawny kid shaped like a question mark bellowed again into his face: "Whatta ya think yer doin'?"

I could feel Celeste's hand wrapping itself around my knee under our table, and I clutched at it for no reason other than that Question-Mark Boy's demand wasn't just a question. It was an invitation. Why else would he have two other guys behind him who appeared to have crawled out of the scum of the same gene pool?

I wasn't usually that judgmental, but this trio looked as if it needed to be hosed down BEFORE being allowed inside to shower. Question-Mark Boy was the worst. His no-specific-color hair was yanked into a ponytail that hung down his back like a chewed-up rope, and he was wearing baggy-butt jeans that apparently hadn't seen a washing machine since the last time he slid across a pool hall floor on his backside.

Besides that, the back of his tee shirt read: VOTE WITH BULLETS.

I shivered.

The way his two Back-Up Boys were slinking steadily around to surround Uri, it was obvious this was going to get stupid, if not worse. Yet none of us could seem to just get up and vacate the area. We, like the twenty or so other kids in the courtyard, could only sit and stare with some kind of sick fascination, as if we were waiting for the inevitable train wreck.

Slowly, Uri set his lunch on the concrete table and stood all the way up.

"Get out while you can, Israeli Dude," Trent muttered.

But Uri didn't look like that was his plan at all. It didn't need to be, as far as I could see. Uri was taller than the scrawny kid and definitely heftier, and his face didn't show fear. It didn't show anything. That seething thing under his skin was doing the talking for him.

"You gonna answer my question or what?" Q-M Boy said. "Whatta ya doin'?"

"I am preparing to eat my lunch," Uri said.

Q-M's two side-kicks gave smirks that clearly said, Can't you even speak English?

"You can 'prepare' all you want," Question-Mark Boy said. "You just can't take up three tables doin' it."

He stuck out his forefinger until it almost went up Uri's nostril. Uri didn't flinch. The other two took menacing steps toward Uri as if Q-M Boy had just pointed out that he wasn't allowed to off more than two or three of us during any given lunch period.

"Oh, for heaven's sake," Stevie whispered. "Now, how stupid is that?"

"Who IS that jerk anyway?" Celeste said, in her something-less-than-a-whisper.

Joy Beth grunted and mumbled, "Redneck."

"No kidding. What's his name?"

"Wolf."

"No stinkin' way," Celeste said.

I could see the resemblance. As "Wolf" made his way around so he could talk into Uri's ear from behind, I got a clear view of his face. It was long and pointy and had a V-shaped mouth, which revealed some fairly nasty looking teeth. He obviously hated dentists as much as he did bathtubs. I could also see the wolf tattoo that covered his right arm like a purplish sleeve. I'd always thought of wolves as being noble animals. I decided I didn't think that anymore.

By now, Wolf had his lips very close to Uri's ear, but when he spoke again it was loud enough to be heard down at the beach. Still, Uri didn't even move an eyelid.

"If you think you people're gonna come here an' take over," he said, "think again."

Uri finally moved, enough to pass a long gaze over his family, who were all looking blankly back at him as if they were merely waiting for a cue. All except Hadassah. Her eyes were smoldering. I figured it was all she could do not to jump up and get in Wolf's pointy little face herself. I almost hoped she would.

"It requires three tables for all of us to sit," Uri said. He stated the fact so coldly I shivered again. Celeste was about to squeeze my kneecap off.

"Then, looks like there's just too many of ya'll, don't it?" Wolf said.

Uri's face stiffened. "This I can do nothing about."

"Where do you expect US to sit?" Wolf said.

"Give me a break!" I hissed to the rest of my table. "I've never seen ANY of those guys come out here for lunch before. What's the deal?"

And then Wolf answered my question.

"If me an' my friends—the people that BELONGS here—can't find a place to sit down if we come out here—then, it looks to me like you people that DON'T belong here need to find some other place to park."

With that, Wolf's goon squad made the last threatening move on Uri they could make without touching him. They didn't have to. I imagined their breath was probably enough to asphyxiate Uri where he stood.

"You deaf?" one of them said. He was wearing a Confederate flag bandana around his head and had a scruffy goatee that made me think about head lice.

"Quentin," Joy Beth muttered. "Idiot."

"Ya think?" Celeste said.

Uri moved only enough to put his eyes on a level with Wolf's. "No, I am not deaf. I can hear you."

"Yeah, but you ain't understandin', there, Hussein," Wolf said. He flashed his yellowed canines. "Else you'd be gettin' your butts movin'."

I wrenched my knee away from Celeste and tried to stand up. She shoved me down by one shoulder, and Joy Beth held me down by the other. Trent's face was pasty.

"Honey, what are you thinkin'?" Stevie whispered to me.

"We can't just let them run people out of here!" I whispered back.

Joy Beth looked uncertainly from Celeste to me. "You want me and Trent to go over there?"

"No!" Stevie and Celeste said together.

I knew we were getting loud, but nobody else in the courtyard was even giving us a glance. They were riveted on Uri, who was nose to nose with Wolf. He had both Quentin and the other Bubba shooting imaginary bullets into his ears with their squinty little blood-shot eyes.

"My family and I are students at this school," Uri said. "We have a right to eat our lunch in this place without harassment." He continued in a flat-line voice. "You may be students in this school as well, but you do not have the right to ask us to remove ourselves. Please step away."

"What you gon' do if we don't?" Quentin said. He was actually licking his lips, as if he were relishing the prospect of taking a bite out of Uri's right ear.

But Wolf put up a hand that stopped Quentin in mid-lick and gave Uri one final slit-eyed look. His voice came out in a low growl.

"You gon' be real sorry you messed with me, man," he said. "You gon' be REAL sorry."

Wolf flipped his skinny self around and led his cronies across the courtyard toward the door. Quentin looked like he'd rather leave a T-bone uneaten. When they got to the exit, he turned around and tried to meet Uri's eyes again, but Uri was already opening a container and examining its contents while his cousins looked on as if they were holding one communal breath. The only person still watching Wolf and the others was Hadassah.

"Freakin' terrorist," Quentin hissed at her.

Then he spat on the patio and slunk away.

There was a sudden frozen silence in the courtyard, which thawed immediately as the various groups turned in on themselves and buzzed like hives. Ours was no exception.

"Tell me again why we eat here instead of going out?" Stevie said.

"I don't get it," Celeste said. "Why did he keep calling Uri 'Hussein'?"

"'Cause he's ignorant." Joy Beth's entire sentence was one big grunt. "He's my cousin's stepbrother. My uncle kicked him out 'cause he's so ignorant. He's the one that drives that truck."

"Which one drives a motorcycle?" Trent said.

"Don't none of them drive a motorcycle."

Celeste nudged her. "Who was the dude that didn't say anything?"

"Joe Philip Morris," Joy Beth said. "They just call him Philip."

"I'd just call him Jerk," Celeste said.

I put both hands up to the sides of my face. "I don't care WHAT their names are!"

Everybody got quiet—including the kids at the next table who gave me a momentary stare before they returned to their own versions of what had just gone down.

"What gives, Duffy?" Celeste said.

I swallowed hard inside my dry, closed-up mouth. I was ready to pry those stupid wires out with my fork.

"What just happened in here," I said, "was heinous."

Trent nodded. "I'm with Stevie. I say we start going to the mall to eat."

"No!" I said—although it came out sounding like one long, whiney NNNNNNNN.

"Duffy, Honey, don't hurt your jaw," Stevie said.

But Celeste shook her head at her, chopsticks wobbling. "Forget it—she's got that look again. G'head, Duff', dish. What's goin' on?"

I pressed my fingers to my forehead. "I don't even know. I just feel horrible that we all just sat here and let those guys get away with that. Nobody even tried to help."

"But they didn't 'get away with it,'" Stevie said. "Uri didn't back down and they left, and his family is sitting there having their lunch." She leaned further across the table, loose curls falling over her shoulders.

"You heard what Hadassah told us—there was so much violence where they lived in Israel, they had to come here to escape with their lives. This was probably nothing to them."

Joy Beth gave a particularly deep grunt.

Celeste poked her. "What, J.B.?"

"They'll be back," Joy Beth said. "This isn't the end of it."

"How do you know?" Stevie said.

I slapped my hands on the table top, concrete stinging my palms. "Hello! Did the rest of you miss that nice little loogey Quentin left for Hadassah?"

"Not to mention the fact that Wolf Boy threatened Uri," Celeste said.

Trent turned to Joy Beth, who was only inches from his face anyway. "Will Wolf make good on that threat?"

She nodded. "If he don't, Quentin will. He's been gettin' in fights since he could walk."

"How do you KNOW these people?" Stevie said. "I've lived here all my life and that's the first time I've ever even heard their names."

"Quentin's my second cousin," Joy Beth said.

Stevie put a well-manicured hand to her mouth. "I'm sorry. We're talking all bad about your family."

"My mama and daddy won't let him on our property."

Trent looked relieved. I knew he spent a lot of time over at the Barnes's.

"Tell me you aren't related to Phillip the Jerk, too," Celeste said.

"Next door neighbor," Joy Beth said. "'Till my daddy caught him tryin' to stuff my brother into the deep freeze on our back porch."

Stevie was gasping.

"He told Philip's daddy if they didn't move, he was gon' call the cops."

"Did they move?" Celeste said. Her blue eyes looked absolutely fascinated.

Joy Beth nodded. "Phillip's daddy was already on parole. He didn't need no more trouble."

"Sweet Jesus," Stevie whispered. I knew she meant it as a prayer. When it came to running to God with every little thing, she and I were neck-and-neck.

Celeste was slowly shaking her head. "It's amazing how good you and your brothers and sisters turned out," she said to Joy Beth. "I mean, I know you have great parents, but just having to deal with people like that at family reunions and stuff –"

Her voice trailed off. I wasn't sure whether she, like me, was just remembering that Joy Beth had spent some time in Juvie before we'd met her. J.B. always said swimming and us and, now, God, were what kept her from putting herself back there.

I shook my head. "I just don't think God wanted us to sit here and let those thre—"

"Rednecks," Trent put in.

"I think we were supposed to at least say something. I could feel it."

"And you'da like to got your jaw broke on the OTHER side," Joy Beth said.

"Like you would have sat here and let them hurt me."

"No stinkin' way!" Celeste said. "We'd have dog-piled 'em!"

I turned my eyes full on her. "What's the difference between protecting ME, and protecting THEM?"

I nodded toward the Dayan family, who were scraping the insides of their lunch containers and wiping their mouths, wordlessly, with passive expressions on their faces. All except Hadassah, who was sitting close to Uri, her lips to his ear, speaking as if she were poking something sharp into it. He was statue-still.

Every girl at my table opened her mouth, eyes full of explanations, and then closed it. Trent blinked in that contact-lenses-out-of-control thing that kicked in when he was extremely uncomfortable.

"So—you want to do something about it, Honey?" Stevie said.

Trent gave her a nudge. "Don't ask her that. It's dangerous, because you know whatever it is, we'll all end up doing it because it'll be right."

"Don't worry about it," I said, "because I have absolutely no idea."

Then with my eyes I followed Hadassah as she made a rapid, stiff-legged exit from the courtyard.

chapterfour

I was unsettled in my afternoon classes.

In Music Theory, my absolute favorite class, it was all I could do to keep my mind from drifting from Mr. Howitch's explanation of syncopated rhythm right back to Hadassah looking straight into the eyes of that scrawny little creep who called her a "freakin' terrorist." When Mr. Howitch asked me to stay after class for a minute, I was sure he was going to start pulling at his nose and get onto me about not paying attention. He had a whole separate language he could "speak" just through mannerisms he did with his beak.

I crept up to his stool where he was perched, as usual, like a small, mustached bird, eyes bright and all-seeing. I had an "I'm sorry" already on my lips when he said, "I miss you too much at rehearsals, Laura. I want you there."

I tried not to SHOW that I was about to melt into a puddle of relief and pointed to my jaw.

"I know, I know," he said. "I personally think you could have pulled off a role with your jaw wired shut and your hands tied behind your back and every other thing."

"No way," I said. I could feel my already-ruddy cheeks doing that blush thing that tended to make me look like a sunburned chipmunk.

"And don't give me any of that stuff about you being just a singer and not an actor," he went on. "That's yesterday's garbage. I want you on my stage." His eyes twinkled at me. "How would you like to sweep it?"

"Excuse me?" I said.

"No reason I can see why you can't be on stage crew if you want to. I need you in my theater as often as I can get you there. Unless, of course, you want to spend your afternoons at the beach…"

I didn't even have to think about it. I grinned until I was sure he could see tidbits of Mom's cottage cheese thing still clinging to my braces.

"I would love to!" I said.

"See you at 2:30 then. I like the stage swept before we start rehearsal. Then you can sit with the stage manager and get notes on set changes. We won't start working with those for a couple weeks yet, but I want you to have a head start since you haven't worked crew for me before."

I nodded happily. I would have scrubbed toilets for that man.

I was in the theater before any of the actors and had the floor swept and the notes from the stage manager copied into my notebook before Mr. H. even called places for a walk-through of the first few scenes. He wrinkled his nose at me—which was Howitch for: "Nice work." I wrinkled mine back and settled in to watch the rehearsal.

The first several minutes were fairly rocky, especially since people were still on-script and getting used to their blocking. There wasn't that much real acting going on yet.

And then K.J. made her entrance. The minute she rushed onto the stage crying, "What'll we do? The village is out!" I found myself sitting further and further forward in my seat.

There was no script in her hand. She moved from place to place without hesitation. And yet the character she was playing—the frightened Mary Warren—was so different from K.J.'s own personality, I had to keep blinking.

That's K.J.? I thought. I watched her allow the girl playing the fierce Abigail Williams to back her into a corner, where Mary Warren cowered and whined, "I never done none of it, Abby! I only looked!"

It would have been more like K.J. herself to be the one saying, "Oh, you're a great one for lookin', aren't you, Mary Warren?" But this girl I was watching, even in the first rough run-through of the scene, was not K.J. O'Toole at all.

She was better than anybody up there, even the seniors, as far as I was concerned, and I had to force myself not to clap when the scene was over and Mr. Howitch climbed up onto the stage.

That must be why she was so grouchy today in group, I thought. She's throwing everything she has into this.

I decided to tell Celeste that at my first opportunity. Otherwise, the two of them were likely to start snatching each other bald-headed.

I didn't call Celeste until I got all my homework done that night, because I knew once we got started talking it could go on for decades. Especially after that day's confrontation in the courtyard. She and I hadn't had a chance to process it yet, just the two of us. I loved the whole bunch of them, but Celeste was definitely my best friend and nothing was quite real until we'd hashed it out at least forty-seven ways.

"Celeste's your BFF," my little sister Bonnie had told me not long before that, her blue-gray, innocent eyes wide and solemn.

I was almost afraid to ask. She'd been coming home from first grade with some pretty interesting phrases lately.

"What's a BFF?" I said.

She rolled the eyes at me. "Du-uh," she said. "Best Friend Forever."

I was too relieved to laugh.

I was just about to dial my BFF's number that evening when the phone rang right under my hand and I jumped about six feet. That was only one of the reasons Pastor Ennis was able to catch me off guard after I said, "Hello?"

"Laura?" he said. Like that was a tough guess. Who else in my house currently spoke as if she had a mouth full of cotton? "Eric Ennis."

I didn't even have a chance to register an uh-oh before he was plunging forward.

"I was so impressed with you the other night," he said. "All of ya'll, actually, but you in particular. I know you've had leadership experience."

"Yes, sir," I said.

He gave a soft laugh. "I've had a lot of it myself, but I guess you could tell it hasn't been with teenagers."

How did you respond to something like that? Yeah, you pretty much stunk at it. He didn't give me a chance to get a word out anyway.

"I don't have to tell you I'm floundering with this, but I just think it's so important for us to have a youth group here at the church. It's just petered out over the last few years from what I understand, and I've spent my whole first year here putting out fires the ADULTS had created—but it's time for me to focus on the youth, and I just wondered—Laura, would you be willing to help get this thing off the ground?"

"Uh, sure," I said. It came out of my mouth automatically. I didn't have much of a history of one-on-one conversations with pastors, but I guessed you didn't say no to them.

"That is wonderful." I could almost see the relief-sweat pouring down his nose already. "Why don't I put you in charge of the program for the next meeting, then? I'm sure those great kids you brought with you would help you. Looked like they'd do just about anything for you."

Oh, yeah, I thought. *They'd be happy to cut my heart out for volunteering them for this.* I hoped he thought the next fifteen seconds of stammering I did were from my wires.

"A week from this coming Wednesday, then?" he said.

"Sure," I said. "That'll be—swell."

"God bless you," he said—and then hung up before I even got my good-bye formed.

I didn't call Celeste. I went straight to the computer. Owen was waiting for me on-line.

> BEACH DUFFY: I just did a stupid thing.
> HAIR: If you did it, it can't be stupid.
> BEACH DUFFY: I let our pastor talk me into organizing a youth group.
> HAIR: that was stupid.
> HAIR: LOL
> BEACH DUFFY: You aren't helping!
> HAIR: If anybody can do it, you can.

❊　❊　❊

Needless to say, most of my FF's did NOT smile at me when, the next day at lunch, I told them what I'd volunteered us for.

"What do you mean, 'us'?" Trent said.

Celeste stared at me.

Joy Beth, of course, grunted.

Only Stevie reacted with even a grain of enthusiasm.

"I have been so bored since everybody that's left on Student Council decided to curl up and sleep the rest of the school year. They're totally apathetic."

"They miss Gigi and Vance and them," Celeste said. "Poor babies."

I started to laugh—nobody could do sarcasm like Celeste—but my eye caught on Hadassah, headed for the three tables where her brother and some of her cousins were already opening their lunches.

Stevie leaned toward me. "I wish we could get somebody like her on Student Council. That would get something going."

"Don't you have to be an American citizen to be on Student Council?" Celeste said.

"What?" Trent squinted at her and shook his dark head. He was having his usual bad hair day, which made the whole exchange look like a scene from a lame sit com.

"Invite her to eat lunch with us," I said suddenly.

"Are you serious?" Stevie said.

"You want to talk to her about Student Council, right?"

"I do. I'm just not sure she'd—"

"Oh, for Pete's sake," Celeste said. She raised her buns halfway off her bench and waved her arm, bologna sandwich still in hand. "Hey— Hadassah!" Her voice always went even deeper when she yelled. "Come sit over here!"

I didn't expect the buzz that suddenly zinged across the courtyard. Two freshmen girls who always hung out on a corner bench got up and left as if a panty raid had just been announced.

As for Hadassah, she glanced warily at her family and then slowly approached us.

"She's coming!" Stevie whispered to me. For no reason I could figure out, her hand went clammy on my arm.

I scooted over to make room for Hadassah, but she stopped behind Trent and shifted her backpack on her shoulder.

"Thank you," she said. "But I will be eating with my family."

"Y'know what they say, though," Celeste said. "You can't pick your family, but you CAN pick your friends." She patted the space I'd made. "Hang out with us."

Hadassah's velvety eyebrows shot up. "My family ARE my friends," she said. "Thank you, but I must decline."

"You sure she's speakin' English?" Joy Beth said when she was gone.

"I'm sorry, but I think that's just plain snotty." Celeste motioned with her sandwich, bologna flapping out the sides. "I was even gonna offer her half."

"I doubt she'd eat it," Trent said. "They only eat kosher."

"Pickles?" I said.

Celeste shook her head. "It's a special way they prepare food so everything's clean and they don't put anything that isn't pure into their bodies or somethin'." She grinned. "I used to give my Jewish friends up in New York hot dogs all the time 'cause their parents wouldn't."

"I don't want nothin' to do with that religion," Joy Beth said, and went back to gnawing on a piece of her mom's fried chicken. I could see the grease glistening on the crispy batter.

"What about OUR religion?" I said. "You guys gonna help me with this youth group or what?"

"Of course, Sugar!" Stevie said. "Let's meet at McDonald's tonight and start planning. I've got a whole book of ice breakers—"

"Okay," Celeste said. "I could use some decent fries."

Joy Beth nodded, and Trent did because she did.

I should have felt one of those I-really–love-my-friends glows right about then, but I couldn't keep my eyes from wandering over to Hadassah. She currently had her arm around her little sister, Nava, who seemed to have just shown up and was crying against Hadassah's chest. Uri said something to them, and Hadassah hissed at him, and he shut up.

Yeah, I bet you don't mess with Hadassah, I thought. *Maybe it was better that she hadn't joined us. No telling what she and Celeste could get into.*

We met at Micky D's that night for a study break, about 8:30. I had a 9:30 curfew on school nights—that was when the oatmeal would be ready—so I hoped we could pretty quickly come up with something that wouldn't act as a youth group sleeping aid.

It turned out to be remarkably easy to plan for some ice breakers—Stevie did have a book called *150 Ways To Get People Talking*—and refreshments. We went with a whole "thawing-out" theme. Celeste said her dad fixed cars for a guy who made ice sculptures who would do one for us for free and we could all smash it at the end of the meeting. That part came from Joy Beth AND Celeste. "It's symbolic," Celeste said.

Stevie just said, "Whatever."

The only thing we were still stressing over at 9:25 was a program.

"Something that means something," I said. "You know, a spiritual thing that we can actually use in our real lives."

"So I guess a speaker on how to change out your carburetor is out of the question, huh?" Celeste said. "My dad could get that for us for free too."

"We still have plenty of time," Stevie said, bouncing her curls around. She was definitely in her element. "Some of the best ideas come when you aren't even looking for them. That's the way it always was in cheerleading and all."

"You ever miss all that popularity stuff, Stevie?" Celeste asked her when we were on the take-everybody-home route in the Expedition.

"I miss the rush of it," Stevie said. "I don't miss the people. Don't get me wrong—not all cheerleaders and Student Council members are snotty and evil, but it doesn't take but one or two in the group who are, and they can poison the whole thing. That's why I got out of everything except Student Council. AND that's why I'm not dating for now. I don't need popularity like I thought I did."

I didn't say so, but Stevie was always going to be "popular." She still couldn't walk two feet down the halls at school without three people saying, "Hey, Stevie!"

Instead, I looked up at the route she was taking, down Harrison Avenue past 'Nama Beach High, and groaned.

"Do we have to go by the school? It reminds me that I have at least two more hours of homework to do before I go to bed."

"Hate it for ya," Stevie said. "Is it chemistry?"

I started to nod—and then I gasped, along with everyone else in the car, including Trent.

We were passing 'Nama, and there across the front of the administration building, spray-painted in distorted red letters were the words: GO HOME, TERERISTS.

Stevie turned on her signal and hung a left across Harrison and onto the shoulder on the school side of the road. Her headlights shone on the building, casting a naked, eerie glow on the message that made me wrap my arms around myself.

"What's that one word?" Joy Beth said.

"Somebody's attempt to spell 'terrorists'," Trent said. "Let's get out of here, Stevie."

But Stevie was digging in her purse and pulled out her cell phone. "We have to get the police."

"Good call," Celeste said. I heard her seatbelt unfasten as she stuck head and shoulders across the console between Stevie and me. "Maybe those punks are still around someplace and the cops can pick 'em up. The paint's still wet—look at that, it's dripping all down the wall. It looks like blood."

I pulled my knees against my chest. "I think that's the idea," I said.

"Yes, sir," Stevie was saying into the phone. "It looks like it just happened –"

"Tell 'em the paint's still running," Celeste whispered.

"—no, I don't see any—"

"Stevie! Over there!"

Celeste threw herself practically onto the dashboard, stabbing her finger against the windshield. "Tail lights!"

I squinted where she was pointing, though all I could see were two faint smears of red receding into the dark. I actually didn't need to see, because I could hear tires squealing like hit dogs out from behind a row of dumpsters.

And then I did see—one more tail light, streaming off after them to the unmistakable rhythm of a motorcycle.

"Tell the police!" I said to Stevie.

"I already hung up. Let me hit redial—"

"No—let's go after them!" Celeste bolted for the backseat again and thrust herself from the waist up out the side window. "They're heading down Magnolia. You can catch them, Stevie!"

"The police said to stay here!"

"Leave Duffy for them—the rest of us'll follow—"

"What?" I said.

"I am SO not going after them, Celeste!" Stevie said. "My daddy would kill me!"

Celeste hauled herself back into the Expedition's backseat. "If we had MY car we'd be going after them. We'da nailed them by now."

"And done what with them?" Trent said.

Celeste set her chin. "Held them until the cops got there."

"Oh, uh-HUH," Stevie said. She turned so she could look right at Celeste. "I'd just pull this $45,000 vehicle right in front of them and let them T-bone me. Then my daddy would kill me again."

"He wouldn't have to," Trent said. "We'd be dead already."

"You'd never catch 'em anyway."

We all looked at Joy Beth. She had slumped down in the seat and had her arms folded across her chest.

"You mean, if it's who we're all thinking it was," I said.

Joy Beth shook the panels of hair out of her face. "I know who it was."

"Come on, J.B.," Celeste said. "Even I couldn't tell the make of that vehicle from here. It sounded like a V-8, but I don't think it was bangin' on all eight—"

"It's not that," Joy Beth said. She nodded toward the graffiti. "There's nobody else at this school that spells that bad."

Stevie tapped at her lips with her nails. "So do we tell the police we think it was Wolf and them?"

"No," Trent said.

Celeste leaned all the way across Joy Beth to get near his face. "Why the heck not?"

Trent's skin was already blotchy, and his eyes were blinking at warp speed, but he shot right back at her with, "Because we don't know. All we've got is that whoever did it failed fifth grade grammar."

Joy Beth narrowed her eyes at him. "I DO know."

"Fine. You going to say that to the police?"

"No," Joy Beth said. She looked at me. "I thought Duffy would."

"What do we do?" Stevie said to me. "You always know, Laura."

Celeste pulled her nose out of Trent's face and put it in mine. "Is God telling you anything right now?"

"For Pete's sake!" I said. My voice was spiraling up into some cavity in my head. "It's not like I've got Him on speed dial!"

Blue lights were suddenly flashing through the back windows. But Celeste, Joy Beth, Stevie, even Trent, were watching me, and in the in-and-out-glare I could see in their eyes the expectation Stevie had voiced: You always know, Laura.

I wish I DID have you on speed dial, God! I thought. There was no tugging at me, though—which just meant, You don't need any special instructions. Do what you already know.

"The truth is the only way to go," I said. "We should tell them exactly what we saw and heard."

"No theories, then," Trent said.

He looked at Joy Beth. She glared at him. THAT wilted him.

"Can I use your cell phone, Stevie?" I said. "I'm way past curfew."

While the two police officers started questioning everybody, I called Dad. He was standing there beside me almost before I pushed the END button and wiped the sweat off Stevie's phone. I hoped he'd remembered to turn off the burner under the oatmeal.

There was no need to worry. He had me interviewed by the police and out of there before it even got cold. When we got home, I still didn't slurp up much of it with B.B.'s syringe—I was too busy telling Dad what happened. Across the kitchen table, he nodded through most of it, and I had to give him credit, he only looked like he wanted to say, Laura, please stay as far away from this as you can three or four times.

However, when I finally wound down, he did tell me to go straight to bed—no computer—because I looked "haggard." I hoped Owen would understand.

But I wasn't sure WHAT I understood. I lay in bed in the dark with my window open for a long time, feeling the night-muggy air and smelling the gardenias and trying not to sort so much that I'd miss something from God. I'd been known to do that.

As I let things rain down on me, they seemed to fall into two puddles.

One was the Celeste/Joy Beth puddle. Let's DO something about this! Let's go after those punks. Let's tell everybody that we know they're out to get the Israeli kids, like they haven't made it that obvious already. These "Rednecks" could be dangerous. We have to stand up for Hadassah and her family.

The other was the Stevie/Trent puddle. Yes, they ARE dangerous, so let's stay out of it. Those Israeli kids have already shown they're not going to be run out by a bunch of skinny little losers who can't find their way to the Laundromat. They obviously don't want our friendship, let alone our help. Let's just leave it alone.

I had a foot in each puddle.

I had been the one who had wanted to stand up in the courtyard and yell for Wolf and his runt-pack to back off. That had felt like a definite tug. And it had been me who had told Stevie to invite Hadassah over to our table, an impulse that had simply come to me.

But I was also the one who had broken out into major perspiration when the police drove up. Nobody else had called her daddy to come to her rescue except me. And didn't I have to admit that I had been thinking what Trent hadn't said when he'd told us not to express any theories to the police: If you start pointing fingers at people who had no qualms about stuffing a small child into a chest freezer, you are likely to have a misspelled message on the front of your house very soon.

I shuddered at the thought of my parents waking up to red spray paint on pink stucco. But I couldn't settle comfortably into an image of watching the Dayan family being chased across the Florida/Alabama border by a large, noisy vehicle with a V-8—whatever that was—either.

I tried to get peaceful, tried to listen. All I could hear were tires squealing and bad grammar being spewed from between yellow teeth.

I toyed with the keys on the bracelet I almost never took off, the one Mrs. Isaacsen gave me and had been adding to every few months. One unlocked the power of surrender, the other the power of discipline. They had opened doors I didn't even know God had created. I'd used them both tonight, and I was still standing out in a hallway looking at doorknobs.

There was usually only one way to start finding the way in. I had to talk to Mrs. Isaacsen about another key.

chapterfive

When I got to school the next morning, there were already men sandblasting the front of the school, and the G and the O were history.

The tension inside the building wasn't so easily erased. It was the way it felt when there was a rumor afoot that there was going to be a major fight at the lockers at an appointed time. No one talked out loud about it, but it was in every whisper, every glance over the shoulder, every jump when somebody slammed a locker too hard.

When Hadassah walked into second period, everybody who was already in the room seemed to suck in breath at once and wait, as if they were expecting her to make a public statement for her family.

"Oh, for heaven sake," Stevie whispered to me.

She reached out, took Hadassah by the forearm, and was able to pull her over to our desks before she went stiff. I was glad Stevie let go about then. Hadassah had steam coming out of her emotional pores.

"I don't know what they think they're looking at," Stevie said, loud enough for "they" to all hear it. "They" quickly found other things to occupy themselves.

"That was kind of you," Hadassah said. Her voice was like a board. "But I do not need—"

"I needed to do it," Stevie said—her own voice hardening a tad. "It's all about me."

If Hadassah caught the sarcasm, she didn't show it.

"Are you guys okay?" I said. "You and your family?"

Hadassah all but rolled her eyes at me. "We have had friends murdered by terrorists—Hamas suicide bombers,," she said. "A few words scrawled on a building do not crush me." She was pretty good at sarcasm herself. "In fact, I am not sure that message was intended for us. We do not know this word 'tererist.'"

"Oh, see, that's because the people that did it spelled it wrong," I said. "They meant—"

"She knows what they meant, Laura," Stevie said. Her eyes, usually so soft, were shooting word-bullets at Hadassah. "You know, we aren't like a lot of people. We really would like to be friends with you, only you act like you don't even want any friends. If you don't, just say so and we'll leave you alone."

"I don't," Hadassah said.

"All right then," Stevie said. And then her eyes went mushy and she said, "But why? I just don't understand that."

"You would not, of course."

"Okay," I said, "so why don't you explain it to us?"

Hadassah looked from one of us to the other without moving her head. "If I do," she said finally, "will you then leave me in peace?"

"Maybe," Stevie said.

She patted the seat of her desk, and Hadassah sank slowly into it. I sat in mine and Stevie grabbed an empty one and pulled it over. Hadassah gave the top of the desk a heavy look.

"I suppose I must start from the beginning," she said. "You know nothing of our conflict in Israel."

"We know the basics," Stevie said, glancing at me. "Okay, so after World War II, the UN divided Palestine into a Jewish state and a Palestinian state, only the Palestinians and the Arab states said no way and invaded to drive the Jews out."

I nodded, although I wasn't sure I could have put that much together.

"Then—let me see if I can remember this—the Jews defended themselves and kept their original state, but the Palestinians never actually got a state because Jordan and Egypt controlled—what's it called?"

Hadassa twitched an eyebrow. "The West Bank and the Gaza Strip. And we—the state of Israel, acquired those territories in a war of self defense—much later—in 1967. But the Palestinians do not just want the West Bank and the Gaza—they want the complete destruction of Israel."

The heat was shimmering off of Hadassah as she spoke, as if the Palestinians were at that moment lurking in the hallway at 'Nama High. I even glanced nervously in that direction myself.

Hadassah leaned in. "Do you know why Israel was given to us—given back to us?"

"Because God promised it to you?" I said.

Surprise flickered through Hadassah's eyes. I could almost hear her saying to herself, Who would have thought she had a brain in there? I tried not to shoot a couple of bullets at her myself.

"That is correct," Hadassah said.

Stevie twirled a strand of hair around her finger. "From what Mr. Beecher has told us, those territories are just two little pieces of land—"

"You look on the map and it's, like, the size of two neighborhoods. What is the big deal?"

"If you knew what was in the West Bank, you could not ask that."

"What?" Stevie said.

"Jerusalem," Hadassah said.

I sat up straighter in the chair.

"Our temple," Hadassah said, pressing her hand against her chest. "The First Temple was built there by Solomon, and the Second as well. All that remains of it is the Western Wall." She looked accusingly at me. "You Gentiles call it the Wailing Wall. We do not. It is a sacred place for us, as are many in Jerusalem."

"So are the Palestinians just being evil about it?" Stevie said.

Hadassah looked as if she would like to say yes. For the first time, she lowered her eyes. "From the Wall, you can see the Dome of the Rock, still close by."

"Which is?"

"The oldest Muslim shrine still in existence." Hadassah spoke as if she could barely stand to say the words. "It is their belief that Muhammad ascended to heaven from there."

I squirmed in my seat. "Okay, they ARE just buildings, right? I mean, you can worship anywhere—at least, that's what we believe."

Hadassah's head came up again. Her eyes took on heat as she looked at me.

"Do you know what else stands in Jerusalem?"

"I don't—"

"The Church of the Holy Sepulcher. It honors the place where your Jesus Christ was crucified. In the nearby town of Bethlehem, also in the West Bank, is the Church of the Nativity. This is traditionally regarded as the spot where your Jesus was born. Would you like to be told you cannot go there and pay honor to your great teacher, who you believe to be the Son of God? Would it be so easy for you to say, 'Oh, it is no big deal, they were just buildings,' if Hamas terrorists destroyed them with bombs?"

I suddenly felt somebody behind me. Mr. Beecher was standing over us.

"I hate to interrupt," he said, his voice low. "But class has started."

I looked around. Every other head except ours was bent over a piece of paper. There was a pop-quiz silence in the room.

"I really do hate to stop you," he said as he handed each of us a half a printed sheet. "It sounds like you were actually having an intelligent conversation—or was that just wishful thinking on my part?"

He grinned, but none of us grinned back. As soon as he was gone, Hadassah stood up.

"We have to continue this conversation later," Stevie whispered to her. "Because I still don't understand what all of this has to do with you not wanting to be friends."

"I don't know if you CAN understand," Hadassah said, and wove her way among the desks to an empty seat in the back.

"Maybe I don't WANT to understand now," Stevie said under her breath.

I just turned to the pop quiz. I wasn't sure. I wasn't sure at all.

In group that day, Mrs. I. put aside the powerful-and-powerless discussion we were supposed to have so we could "express our feelings" about the graffiti, since that was all anybody was talking about anyway.

"Tell where you stand if you want," Mrs. I. said. "Ask questions if you want. No fixing. No cross talk. No negatives."

We all sat there like we'd been stricken with sudden laryngitis.

"That killed that discussion," Celeste said brightly. She was wearing camouflage pants and an olive-drab Tee-shirt. The only thing missing was the face paint. Subtlety wasn't exactly Celeste's strongest characteristic.

"We can say what we honestly think, right, Miz I.?" Stevie said.

"As long as you stay within the rules."

"Then I think that kind of hate is just WRONG."

"Why can't we all just get along?" K.J. muttered.

"Excuse me?" Mrs. Isaacsen said.

"Nothing," K.J. said.

She leaned her head back and closed her eyes, and I looked twice at her. This was definitely un-K.J.-like behavior.

That looks like something Mary Warren would do, I thought. *Maybe she's just in character all the time now.* Strangely, I missed the barbs and baiting questions the real K.J. always tried to get away with, all the while grinning at Mrs. I. like a five-year-old with her hand in the Twinkie drawer.

"I'm just waiting to see what those Israeli kids are gonna do about it," Celeste was saying.

"You're certainly dressed for the occasion," Mrs. I. said dryly. "What—no combat boots?"

"I outgrew mine," Celeste said. She wrinkled her nose-freckles.

"I have a feeling the Israelis aren't going to do anything about it," I said. "Hadassah said they've seen a lot worse things than that."

"I don't get it."

Mrs. I. looked over the tops of her half glasses at Joy Beth. "What don't you get, J.B.?"

"If somebody does something to my family, my family stands up for theirselves. If we didn't, half of us probably wouldn't even be alive."

The image of one her wide-faced little brothers with a freezer lid coming down on him flashed through my mind.

"Do you want to speak to that, Michelle?" Mrs. I. said. "Your people have certainly had to make some of those decisions."

"You mean my family, or my race?" Michelle said. She pressed her very full lips together.

"Your race."

Michelle re-crossed her legs and smoothed her palms over the black skirt that fit her like a business executive's. "Dr. King believed in passive resistance," she said. "I s'pose it's helped us, I don't know."

"Question," Celeste said.

Mrs. I. nodded her on.

"You don't think you—meaning black-people—got helped? I mean, don't you feel equal to white people now?"

I expected Michelle to give her usual, Do I have to answer that question?, but to my surprise, she leaned forward, her hands on both panty-hosed knees. Not a strand of her curved black hair moved as she spoke.

"There's times I don't feel equal—like when I take my—when I go to the clinic and I get a white doctor and he won't even take his eyes up from the file while he's askin' us questions."

"I'd have to get in that doctor's face," Celeste said.

Mrs. I. gave her a warning look.

"Fixing, sorry, my bad," Celeste said.

"It's all good," Michelle said. "I have bigger things to worry about anyway." Then she pulled back into the world none of us knew anything about.

After an unusual silence, Mrs. Isaacsen reached over and patted K.J.'s knee. "You have anything you want to say?"

"I thought sure you'd have a picket line going out there this morning, girl," Stevie said. "Oh—how can I put that in the form of a question?"

"You can't," K.J. said. "So just forget it." She glanced somewhat warily at Mrs. I. before she added, "I'm with Michele. I got bigger things to worry about."

Something inside me bristled. I couldn't quite grasp it, and I wasn't sure I wanted to. But as soon as the bell rang for lunch, I asked Mrs. I. for an appointment.

"I'd love it, Laura!" she said. "But I don't have anything until tomorrow before school." She looked closely at me. "It isn't an emergency, is it?"

"Not yet," I said. And then I laughed.

She gave me one of those I-know-you-Laura-Duffy nods.

When Celeste, Stevie, Joy Beth, and I got to the door that led out to the courtyard, Trent lurched out of nowhere and practically threw himself across the doorway.

"Let's go to the mall and eat," he said. "I'll buy."

"For all of us?" Stevie said. "Sugar, you don't have to do that—"

"No, he doesn't."

We all looked at Celeste. She didn't even need the face paint or the combat boots to look any more like she was going into battle.

"You're just trying to keep us away from what might happen, aren't you?" she said.

Trent's eyelids went into vibration.

"That's what I thought," Celeste said.

"And what's wrong with that?" Stevie said. "I personally don't want to watch another scene—and Hadassah made it VERY clear that she doesn't want our help."

"Uh," Joy Beth said.

Celeste nudged her. "What?"

"She might change her mind when Wolf starts swingin'."

"You think he'd do that?" Celeste said.

"I'm surprised he ain't done it already."

"Then I am definitely outa here," Trent said. He curled his fingers around Joy Beth's forearm. "And you're coming with me."

Joy Beth turned to him in slo-mo and gave him a look so cold I was surprised he could even uncurl his fingers from her arm. Which he did.

Oops, I thought.

"I'll go with you, Trent," Stevie said. "But you are not buying for me. Laura, can you drive? My car's a pig sty."

I looked at the four of them, standing in their two separate puddles. This time, I couldn't keep a foot in each one. I had to jump into one or the other—I just didn't want to drown in whichever one I chose. I closed my eyes.

"If we're going to go, we have to do it now," Trent said. "I can't be late for physics."

"Chill—she's praying," Celeste said.

"I've already prayed about it," Stevie whispered. "And I know Jesus doesn't want me involved in THIS mess." I could hear her keys jingling "I'll let you listen to Jami Smith. I'll even clean off my back seat real quick."

"You won't need your backseat if it's just you and Trent," Celeste said.

I opened my eyes to see Trent's face going blotchy. He looked at Joy Beth as if she were already sawing off his left leg.

Stevie's creamy-latte brow puckered. "You aren't coming, Laura?"

"I don't think so," I said.

"God told you to stay, right?" Celeste said. She gave a triumphant nod.

"No. God's not saying anything," I said. I didn't add, Who could hear Him with you all jacking your jaws? "If I can't hear something clear, then I don't change what I always do."

"She's staying," Celeste said. For the first time, I realized she was wearing a set of dog tags on a long chain, which she pulled out and ran back and forth. I was surprised she didn't start carving a notch on the doorjamb or something.

Stevie shook her head slowly at me. "Sugar, you of all of us can't afford to get hurt again. If you end up with something else broken—your daddy is going to kill you."

"I'll be okay," I said.

"Does she think all fathers are homicidal?" Celeste whispered to me as we pushed through the doors.

I didn't answer. I looked back to see if Joy Beth was following, but she was still standing in the hall, staring at Trent. He looked like Gumby for a minute, stretched to the limit in both directions. Joy Beth didn't wait for him to let go and snap one way or the other. She turned solidly and shoved through the doorway ahead of me.

"You okay, Joy?" I said when we got to our table.

"No," she said.

"Look, every couple fights," Celeste said. She wrinkled her nose at Joy Beth. "Making up is half the fun."

"I didn't think he was a wus."

Celeste pushed Joy Beth's brown bag toward her. "Eat, J.B. I don't want you having an insulin reaction."

Joy Beth looked like she'd rather consume the concrete table.

I nodded toward the Dayans' table. "Trent doesn't know any of these kids. Maybe he doesn't want to put it on the line for people he doesn't even know."

"Yeah, but this is about principle," Celeste said. "Isn't that why you're still here, Duffy?"

I couldn't answer her, because I still had no idea why I was there. God wasn't giving me any definite tugs.

"A'right," Celeste said. "So as long as we're stayin', we need a game plan. You know your militia cousins, J.B.—what do you think they'll do now?"

Joy Beth was staring across the courtyard. "See for yourself," she said.

Pools of perspiration immediately formed in the lines of my palms as I watched Wolf slouch with purpose straight from the door to the bench where Uri was sitting. Quentin and Joe Philip followed several feet behind him again, in a bodyguard sort of way that would have made me laugh under other circumstances. Joy Beth could probably break both of them over her knee like sticks.

"Hey, Hussein," Wolf said. "You ain't packin' yet?"

"Packin' a pistol?" Celeste whispered to us.

"I think he means packing his suitcases," I whispered back.

Uri stood up and stepped away from the bench. He still had the stiff-faced expression that said this was affecting him like a re-run of "The Brady Bunch." But that something beneath his skin simmered up a different story. The sweat puddles in my hands turned to ice-ponds.

"I asked you a question, Hussein. I said 'you ain't packin' yet?'"

"I have already informed you that I am not deaf," Uri said. "I would give you an answer if I understood the question."

My gaze, on its way back to Wolf, snagged on Hadassah. She sat directly in line between them, and she was giving off more steam than her brother. Her eyes were burning a hole in the side of Wolf-Boy's face that I was surprised he didn't feel.

No, actually, I'm not surprised, I thought. *I don't think Wolf-Boy "feels" anything.*

Except maybe his major ego expanding his head like an over-stretched balloon. I expected that ponytail to pop out any minute and spatter the courtyard with oil. The way Hadassah was smoldering, a grease fire was guaranteed.

Meanwhile, the place was starting to fill up as if word had mysteriously filtered out into the hallways that there was about to be a smack-down right there in the courtyard. I glanced toward the cafeteria. It was one big glass wall on the courtyard side, and everyone in there—mostly freshmen and sophomores without cars to escape campus during lunch—had their hands and faces pressed to it.

Where the heck are the administrators? I thought. Dr. Vaughn and Mr. Stennis were usually like the K-9 Corps, there at the first sign of trouble as if they could smell it through the walls. Where were they now?

"What—are you blind in both eyes?" Wolf was saying to Uri. "We left you a message—said, 'GO HOME, TERERISTS.'"

"Ah. That is what it said." Uri nodded as if he'd just had an epiphany—but I'd hung out with Celeste long enough to know sarcasm when I heard it. "I have never seen the word spelled that way."

"What word?"

"'Terrorists.'" Uri twitched an eyebrow, his first facial movement. It was as effective as a poke taken right at Wolf-Boy's eyes. "But I still fail to see how that message could be directed at me."

"At all ya'll!" Wolf said.

His voice cracked, causing a few snickers from the crowd, which Quentin and Joe Philip silenced with a pair of snarls. Even as hard as my heart was pounding, I wanted to snarl back.

"Ya'll are all terrorists that come outa I-Rack."

"Ah." Uri once again pretended to be suddenly seeing the light. Celeste, I could tell, was digging it. "There is your mistake. We are not from Iraq. We are from Israel."

"Same thing—all ya'll raghead Muslims are terrorists, I don't care where you come from."

I caught movement from Hadassah. She was rising from the bench. On either side of her, boy cousins put their hands on her shoulders. She looked as if she wanted with everything that was in her to shake them off. I could feel the heat gathering under her skin, the anger roiling in her head—against the ignorance that was being spewed out above her, down over her, like venom.

"Another mistake," Uri said. His voice was like wood. "We are Jews, not Muslims. There is a vast difference."

"You're a freakin' terrorist, Jew Boy!" Wolf's voice broke again, as if too many cigarettes had rendered his vocal chords brittle. But there was no laughter from the crowd this time. It merely hummed with a ghoulish undertone, and even from across the courtyard, I could see it burning in Hadassah's eyes. Only the hands on her shoulders were keeping her down, I knew that much.

"Who is behaving more like a terrorist here?" Uri said.

It was as if that was the cue Wolf had been waiting for, written on some unseen script he and his two henchmen had composed long before they'd walked out there that day.

"You callin' me a terrorist?" He growled the words out through his teeth and then hurled himself straight at Uri, the heels of his hands connecting with his collarbone and knocking him backwards into the concrete table. Quentin and Joe Phillip were immediately there, jerking Uri up and holding him like a target for Wolf's drawn-back fist. Only Joy Beth's grip kept Celeste in her seat. Only her cousins' hands held Hadassah back. But there was no one restraining me.

Even as a tall guy with a shiny ponytail down his shoulders slipped through the leering crowd and scattered them like so many flies—and even as he deftly ripped the still-flailing Wolf off of Uri—and even as Wolf screamed, "Freakin' Jew called me a terrorist! I ain't no terrorist!"—somebody else was on top of a concrete table, straining to get the words out between teeth that wouldn't come apart.

"What is the MATTER with you people? What is the MATTER with you?"

chapter**six**

I could vaguely hear Celeste yelling, "Go, Duffy! You go, girl!" and I distantly felt Joy Beth plucking me off the table by the back of my shirt. The only thing I was clearly aware of were Hadassah's eyes, boring into me from across the courtyard.

Leave it alone, they said. Just leave it alone.

The crowd was gone as quickly as it had gathered. The Israeli family made no attempt to return to lunches, but folded in on itself, the only audible sound coming from little Nava, who was sobbing uncontrollably.

"Are you freakin' crazy or what?" Joy Beth said to me.

"Why did we stay here, then?" I said. "Just to watch, like everybody else?"

My voice was shaking. My whole body was shaking.

Celeste put both arms around me from behind, and I could feel her heart beating against my back. "No," she said, "but for Pete's sake, Duffy, I thought you were just gonna be over here prayin'—not jumpin' up and down on the table. I mean, I was prouda ya, but you shoulda let me and Joy Beth do the physical stuff." Celeste yanked the dog tags back and forth on the chain. "You were the one on top of the table yellin'. If you didn't mean, 'somebody get out there and stand up for them,' then what the heck were you talkin' about?"

"I don't know yet," I said.

"Beautiful, Duff," Celeste said. "Exquisite."

"At least he was here to break it up," I said.

Celeste and Joy Beth both stared at me. "Who?"

I looked across at the Dayans' table. There were only dark heads bent together over a girl who was crying as if her heart would break.

"I figured the bell just broke it up," Celeste said. "It rang and everybody ran. Come on, Duffy—what's going on with you?"

"I don't know," I said. It was obvious they hadn't seen Ponytail Boy. Maybe I hadn't either. "I just know I felt—something."

"You reckon you could let us know next time you 'feel'?" Joy Beth said.

"Okay," I said. "How 'bout now?"

"Huh?"

I pulled away from Celeste. "I have to go talk to Hadassah. If I'm not back in five minutes, call a posse."

"You don't need no stinkin' posse, man," Celeste said to me, grinning. "You got us."

Joy Beth, of course, grunted.

I was praying like crazy as I tapped one of the cousins on the shoulder and said, "Could I talk to Hadassah, please?"

They parted like the proverbial Red Sea and looked at her. She turned from her little sister to me, irritation practically standing her velvet brows on end.

"Yes?" she said.

"I'm sorry," I said. "About what just happened."

She averted her eyes from me. "You are not responsible for the actions of everyone."

"The rest of us could have done something, though," I said.

The eyes were back on my face. "I told you: we do not need your help."

There was a sudden blurting-out of what I could only guess was Hebrew from Uri. If I hadn't been quaking in my Sketchers, I would have smiled. The tone of brother talking to sister sounded the same in any language. Whatever it was, it made Hadassah flip her hair back and look up at me once again.

"Thank you. We appreciate your—caring." She didn't add 'if that's what it is,' though I could hear it screaming to come out.

"I do care," I said. I glanced back at Joy Beth and Celeste who were nearly falling off the bench. "We—my friends and I—care. We want to do something to help."

"You cannot help because you do not understand."

"Then help us understand—like you started to do second period."

"It is too much—"

"So we'll start small." My mouth was so dry I could hardly squeeze the words out. I hadn't realized until then that the rest of the family was staring curiously at my clenched jaws. Even Nava had stopped crying.

Hadassah didn't look at Uri as he whispered something in her ear. Instead, she let her glance shoot over to Joy Beth and Celeste and dart back.

"All right," she said. "But just you—not all your friends."

I rammed around in my head and grabbed the first choice that raised its hand.

"Okay—but can we do it with another friend—an adult friend—she's my counselor—"

"Mrs. Isaacsen?" Hadassah said.

"Yeah—you know her?"

"Yes. I will talk to you with her."

I should have known, I thought as I told Hadassah to meet me at Mrs. I.'s office the next morning and headed back to the now salivating Celeste and Joy Beth. *Why didn't I just think of that in the first place?*

✳   ✳   ✳

By the time I left rehearsal that afternoon, I really needed some quiet time, just to sort out what was God and what was Ponytail Boy and what was going on in me that was driving me. The weather was perfect for driving out to St. Andrew's Bay State Park, and I'd have given a couple of grade points to climb out into the jetties and sit beside a pelican and hear a God-whisper or feel a God-tug.

But it was too late in the day, so I settled for driving down to Beach Street on the bay and hanging out in the car listening to Jami Smith while I watched a pelican fish from the end of the pier in a sizzle of sunset. There was something about her music, something about the deep, husky way she sang that Christ's love was deeper than my view of grace, wider than the gap He filled. It was perfect, because I did feel a gap. I was missing Owen. I was bugged because I was thinking Richard–thoughts again. And now this thing with Hadassah that wouldn't leave me alone. If only I could sing—that always pulled me out of holes. I hummed, but it wasn't the same.

After Bonnie left the dinner table that night, I brought Mom and Dad up to speed on what was happening at school. Out of respect for our agreement to keep all communication open, I included the part about me getting up on the table, although the large, chicken-hearted side of me wanted to conveniently omit it. After all, I had also agreed to honor any decision they handed down to me when they thought they needed to.

By the time I got to that part, Mom's round, rosy, Bonnie-like face was the color of the sink—a spotless white you could see yourself in.

"For once I'm grateful for those jaw wires," she said. "Probably not that many people heard you, do you think?"

I twisted my mouth a little. "No—and I guess that's okay for now. I don't exactly know what I need to do next anyway. Hadassah and I are meeting with Mrs. Isaacsen in the morning."

"Good," Dad said. "She's a good lady. You listen to her."

"I hope she tells you to let adults handle it," Mom said. "This could be dangerous, Laura. Those people blow themselves up."

"Israelis don't blow themselves up, Mom," I said. "Palestinians do that."

Dad gave me an approving little eyebrow lift.

"Besides," I said, "how can adults 'handle' how kids treat each other? That's what this is about, as far as I'm concerned."

I hadn't really known that piece of it until I'd said it. The talking was helping.

But talking to Stevie on the phone that night didn't help.

"I TOLD you it was gon' be a mess, Sugar," she said. "And then you went and crawled up on the TABLE—"

"Okay, so that was lame," I said. "But at least I got Hadassah to agree to talk about more stuff—and we're doing it with Mrs. I."

"THAT I can handle," Stevie said. "What time do you want us there?"

"Ummmm." I lay back on my bed with the phone, searching the ceiling for tact.

"What?"

"Hadassah said she only wanted me there."

"Oh. Well—okay—I can see that. "

But I was sure she couldn't. Stevie wasn't used to being cut out of things.

After that I asked Mom to "hold my calls." I finished my homework and got online with Owen.

"I'm just going to let the God-rope pull me," I IM'd him.

HAIR: Who's going to be watching your back? Man, I wish I was there.

BEACHDUFFY: I do, too, so you could tell me what I'm doing.

I signed off feeling anxious.

✳ ✳ ✳

Mrs. Isaacsen had the tea on when I joined her and Hadassah the next morning, only it didn't smell like our usual Earl Grey. I sniffed the air. "It's a tea I bought in Israel," Mrs. Isaacsen said. "I thought that would be appropriate."

"Where did you get it?" Hadassah said. It was the first time I'd seen anything but anger or guarded civility in her eyes. Did I detect a faint glimmer of appreciation?

"On my last visit to the Holy Land," Mrs. I. said. "I used to go every couple of years—the year I took my sabbatical I worked on a kibbutz." She gave Hadassah a sad look. "I don't have to tell you that it is far too dangerous for me to make those trips now."

"I understand for you," Hadassah said. "But when it is your home, it is never 'too dangerous'".

The way Mrs. Isaacsen squeezed her shoulder, the way Hadassah looked at her without rage or resentment, I could tell this was the recycling of a conversation they had had before. I felt an odd pang.

Mrs. Isaacsen poured some of the strong-smelling tea into my Metropolitan Opera mug and settled into one of the cushy, nestling chairs. I couldn't keep from looking to see what kind of cup Hadassah. It was white with a gold, six-pointed star on it.

Star of David, I thought. *I know that's a Jewish thing. Dang—Mrs. I.'s already gotten Hadassah her own cup.*

"You know what I did the last time I was over there?" Mrs. I. said. I shook my head.

"I traveled the path of Abraham," she said. "Well, not quite the entire path. Ur, where he was originally from, is in Iraq, and Saddam Hussein was having none of it. He wouldn't even let the Pope go there."

"This I know," Hadassah said.

I nodded as if I did too.

"We had to imagine the ancient cities which no longer exist—Haran, Damascus, Sodom, and Gomorrah."

I made sure I was the first to nod this time. I knew those—well, some of them.

"What I loved," Mrs. I. went on, eyes glowing, "was thinking of Abraham obeying God's instructions without even knowing where they would take him. He had no idea that he was sanctifying holy ground with every step he took."

"OUR holy ground," Hadassah said.

"Ours, too, though, right?" I said. "It's from the Old Testament—we believe in that."

"Yours—ours—" Mrs. I said, pointing to Hadassah and then to me. "And our Muslim brothers and sisters."

"No stinkin' way!" I said.

Hadassah gave me a disdainful look.

"Really?" I said.

"So they think," Hadassah said. She looked at Mrs. I. "May I?"

"Of course—though we don't practice condescension in my office."

Hadassah bowed her head slightly. I smothered a superior smile. Mrs. I. never had to come down on ME like that.

"Muslims look at Abraham as their patriarch as well," Hadassah said to me. "The story they tell in the Koran is much the same as ours, except that we know that it was Isaac, son of Sarah, that Abraham nearly sacrificed to the Lord, and the Muslims believe it was Ishmael, Abraham's son by Hagar, who was—"

"Sarah's handmaiden—" I said quickly.

"Egyptian handmaiden—" Hadassah said.

"—the one she said could have a baby with Abraham because she thought she was too old to have kids—"

"—because she did not trust in the Lord when He said Abraham was to be Father of many nations."

We both looked at Mrs. Isaacsen as if to say, "Who won?"

"Are you two ladies through competing with each other?" she said.

I felt my cheeks turning red all the way up to my eye sockets.

"You'll never come to any kind of understanding until you stop trying to one-up one another."

I didn't deny it. I didn't want Mrs. I. thinking Hadassah was better than me. *Where did THAT come from?* I thought. I know I turned an even deeper shade of red.

Hadassah mumbled, "My apologies."

"The point in all of this is that you two girls, who are each so passionate about your faiths, arise from the same beginning—and so do your Muslim sisters."

I thought Hadassah was going to spit. I was sure if Mrs. I. hadn't been there, she would have.

"But since they aren't part of this equation here," Mrs. I. went on, "we'll leave them out of our discussion."

Good, I thought, *or we're going to need a spittoon.*

"What is it that you want to discuss?" Hadassah said.

She was sitting very straight, very still, and I could feel the heat of whatever seethed beneath her skin. I wasn't sure I wanted to discuss anything with her anymore. But somehow I had to. There was something under my skin too.

Both she and Mrs. I. were watching me, eyebrows uplifted. If I didn't say something, there wasn't going to be a discussion.

"I can't just sit by and let people treat you and your family the way they are," I said. "I just don't know what to do and you tell me you don't want me to do anything, only MY God is saying, 'Do something.'"

"Then why don't you ask Him?" Hadassah said.

"I have. I think that's why I'm here. To talk about that."

"That is what you Americans do so well—talk. You come in and try to make the Jews talk to the Muslims and come to peace." Hadassah's eyes were smoldering. "There can be no peace until they stop the violence."

"That's what I'm trying to find out—how we can stop the violence HERE." I wished I could lick my lips. They felt like the Mojave Desert. "I'm not trying to 'make peace'—this isn't you versus them, it's you versus us, only I'm on your side!"

Hadassah had started shaking her head before I even got the sentence out. "You cannot be on my side. You are a Christian."

"Time out," Mrs. Isaacsen said.

"Why?" Hadassah drew herself up tall in the chair. "She has no idea the hatred that is directed against the Jews. Her people have done as much to us as the Muslims, perhaps more."

"Are you talking about the Holocaust?" I said. "I didn't have anything to do with that! I wasn't even born! Everything I've read about it or seen in movies—it makes me sick to my stomach!"

"How noble," Hadassah said.

"Lose the sarcasm, please," Mrs. Isaacsen said.

Hadassah gave Mrs. I. a long look and then bowed her head. When she looked up, her eyes were cold. "Then I will be direct," she said. She pronounced it dye-rect, which made it feel as if she were about to run me through with a broad sword.

"You cannot tell me that you do not hate the Jews because you think they killed your Christ, even though we, my family and I, were not there at the foot of the cross."

All I could do was stare at her for a moment. And then I shook my head. "I don't hate you. You didn't have anything to do with it. Besides—" I looked at Mrs. Isaacsen, who appeared to be holding her breath. "Jesus was a Jew, wasn't he?"

"He was," Mrs. I. said. "He descended from forty-seven generations of Jews. And he was a good Jew—he taught in the Temple, he observed all the feast days." She turned her eyes on Hadassah. "Our Last Supper was held on your Passover. Our religions are linked together in ways that can't be separated."

Again, Hadassah gave her the respectful nod. "You are the only Christian I have ever met who thinks that way."

I stuck my hand up in the air. "Hello! What am I, chopped liver?"

I sounded so much like Celeste, she might as well have been in the room. Mrs. I. was obviously smothering a smile.

"I am sorry," Hadassah said, without a trace of real remorse in her voice. "I do not know you. How can I trust you?"

"That's what I'm here for! I'm trying to let you know me! And I want to know you."

"She has a point," Mrs. Isaacsen said.

"Why? Why would you care so much?" Hadassah said to me.

"I have no idea," I said.

The eyebrows shot up.

"No—no, I do," I said. "I know that what those guys are doing, the ones who are attacking you, is wrong. And I know that standing by and watching it happen without at least trying to help is wrong. I try to do the right thing, because I can feel God tugging at me."

There was a heavy silence. Mrs. Isaacsen finally said, "Isn't that interesting, Hadassah? I believe those are very similar to the words you said to me yesterday. God is pulling you to go back to your people and try to set things straight."

"And I am frustrated because I cannot do that."

For the first time, something real rose in Hadassah's voice. It held the same heat that exuded from her flesh, and I realized what it was. It was passion. I found myself leaning forward in the chair, my tea gone cold in its mug between my hands.

"Look," I said, "I've never had somebody I loved blown up by a suicide bomber or anything like that, but I know what it feels like to be pulled by God to do something nobody else thinks you should do. On a smaller scale, sure, but—listen—if we both turn to God, and there's only one right thing, doesn't it make sense that He would be telling us the same thing?"

"You are naïve."

"Just because I haven't had the same experiences as you doesn't mean I'm some child," I said. I could feel my cheeks skipping pink and going straight to crimson. "If you don't want me to be naïve, then educate me. Otherwise, I'm just going to do whatever I think is right to try to protect you and your family here at school. Unless you tell me how to help you, I'll probably screw the whole thing up and it'll just get worse."

"Then do nothing. That's how you can help."

"Not an option." I was leaning so far forward I was almost falling out of the chair.

Mrs. Isaacsen reached over and took the mug out of my hands. "Could you sit back in your home in Israel and do nothing?" she said to Hadassah.

"No," Hadassah said. "Not until my father locked me in my room. Just after that, we were brought here."

"There's a war going on in this school right now," I said. "I want it to stop. It's the same thing."

I could see that Hadassah was about to shake her head. I wasn't sure what stopped her—but suddenly she was looking at me, searching my face.

"This," she said. She ran a finger down the side of her jaw. "Was this an injury sustained in the 'war'?"

"Yeah, in a way," I said.

She looked at me some more. "You are not a coward, then."

"No. Which is not to say that I'm not scared to death about half the time."

She did shake her head then. "True courage is doing what is right, no matter what the danger may be. It has nothing to do with having fear or not having fear."

Hadassah's eyes hung onto mine, dark and intense and seeking. I couldn't pull away. I didn't want to. From far away the bell rang, and we each continued to search the other's face until Mrs. Isaacsen said, "This is a good start, ladies. A very good start."

"May I go?" Hadassah said.

"Go in peace," Mrs. Isaacsen said. She put out her hand, but Hadassah ignored it and instead leaned down and kissed Mrs. I. on the cheek before she hurried out. Mrs. I. looked as surprised as I felt.

"I wasn't expecting that," she said. "She's a pretty tough cookie."

"She scares the heck out of me," I said.

Mrs. Isaacsen put her hand on top of mine. "I think she's scared of you, too, Laura. You're a pretty tough cookie yourself."

I sank back into the chair, oblivious to the second warning bell. "I don't think I'm any closer to knowing what to do for them than I was when I came in here. No offense—it's not your fault."

"Darlin', I don't think you can expect to figure out what to do about the unspeakable horrors of 2000 years in a thirty-minute meeting. What I do think is that you're already helping."

"How?"

"You're trying to understand. You keep doing that and I think in time she'll figure out that she can trust you."

"But what if we don't have that kind of time?" I said. "Yesterday at lunch, Wolf and those other two guys out and out threatened Uri, in front of half the school. I don't think he's going to wait around long enough for Hadassah to decide I give a flip about her. Besides—"

I stopped to take a breath. Mrs. Isaacsen watched me closely and then touched my forehead.

"There's a war going on in here too," she said.

"Because I'm also afraid I don't have time to get Stevie and Trent on my side. I know Celeste will help me. If Joy Beth helps it'll probably mean she and Trent will break up." I stopped again and rolled my eyes. "This all sounds so petty compared to what Hadassah has had to face."

"It's where you are. And it's about the same thing."

"Which is?"

"It's about love—no matter what the cost." She smiled as she picked up her frog-shaped pad. "You want some Scripture?"

I nodded.

She didn't even have to consult the Bible to write down chapters and verses. I was convinced she had the entire NIV committed to memory.

"Between now and the time you have a chance to read this," she said, "just respond in love. You can do that, Laura. God won't allow you to do otherwise."

I was still contemplating that on the way to class when I had an idea. I wasn't sure where it came from, which to me was a clear indication that it was a God-thing. I never came up with them on my own. Wherever it had come from, I decided to go with it.

chapter**seven**

"I knew we shouldn't have gone along with this deal," Trent said to Joy Beth.

She pulled a piece of pepperoni off the mini-pizza they were sharing and grunted.

"At least we got her out of that cafeteria," Stevie said.

I raised my hand. "Hello—would you all stop talking about me like I'm not even here?"

"Yeah," Celeste said. "She hates that."

"Besides, a deal's a deal," Stevie said. "Duffy said she'd come to the mall for lunch if we'd agree to her idea."

Trent shook his bad-hair-day head. "We've been railroaded."

"Quit yer whinin'," Celeste said. "It got you and Joy Beth speaking to each other again, didn't it?"

"Maybe," Joy Beth said.

Trent's eyelids began to blink at me. "Okay—so explain to me again what you want us to do."

"Let me do it," Stevie said, "so I'm sure I've got this straight." She shook her curls out of the way. "You want us to ask Hadassah if they'll do a presentation for our youth group about what it's like to be a Jew, and that'll give them a forum and help all of us understand them, and then maybe they'll let us help them—"

"—bring down the Redneck Militia," Celeste said. She was practically licking her chops.

"I'm in, then," Joy Beth said.

"Wait," I said. My eyes were on Trent, who looked like he was about to have a seizure. "I didn't say this was automatically going to lead us into battle. It'll just help us know what we ARE supposed to do."

"There's only one thing Wolf and them understands," Joy Beth said.

"And I'm not going there," Stevie said. "But THIS I'll do. I'll help you get it organized, Duff."

"Me, too," Celeste said. "Only—I think you gotta be the one who asks Hadassah."

"Definitely," Stevie said. "She hates me."

"She doesn't hate you!" I said. "And she's not that crazy about me either."

"Then why are we doing this?" Trent said.

They all looked at me, of course.

"I think," I said slowly, "that it's because we're supposed to respond in love. That's what Mrs. I. said."

"Even if we don't 'love' them?" Trent looked uneasily at Joy Beth. "I'm just being honest. I don't love some guy that all but flips me off."

"I don't know," I said. "It's got something to do with loving God—which we all do, right?"

They nodded, some with more enthusiasm than others.

"That's all I know. I haven't figured the rest of it out yet."

"Let us know when you do," Trent said. He picked up another triangle of pizza.

"Meanwhile, we better get started on planning this youth group thing." Stevie glanced at her watch. "When are you going to ask her, Duffy?"

"If we leave now we can get to her before lunch is over," Celeste said. She was already stuffing half-eaten burgers into a sack.

Trent picked up the whole pizza and held it over his head. "I'm not done!"

"Bring it with," Celeste said. "Let's go."

"Why are you so hyped about this?" he asked.

"Because Duffy is. When has she ever steered us wrong? You ride with me, Duff."

She drove back to the school like we were doing a lap at Nascar. Stevie wheeled in right behind us into the parking lot with Joy Beth and

Trent in her backseat. We all reached the door to the courtyard before the first warning bell rang.

"I hope it's not too late already," Celeste said. "Like, y'know, Wolf has already been out here kicking tail."

Stevie peered through the window in the door. "No, it looks clear."

"It DID."

We followed Joy Beth's nod toward the far end of the hall, where three skinny figures had just made the turn and were slithering toward us. They didn't look like question marks today. They looked like exclamation points.

"You oughta just call her on the phone," Trent murmured to me.

"We can hold 'em off," Joy Beth said. "Won't be easy, but we can do it."

"Isn't anybody coming with me?" I said.

"I would," Stevie said. "But I don't think she'll say yes if I'm there."

"Go, Duffy—before the goon squad starts breathin' down our necks!" Celeste squeezed my shoulder. "We got your back."

Joy Beth pushed the door open, and I squeezed through. The courtyard seemed to hold its breath collectively, but when the scattering of people other than the Dayans saw that it was only me, they turned back to the remains of their corn dogs as if they were disappointed. From the other side of the glass cafeteria wall, the rest of the student body appeared to be doing the same thing.

The only people who seemed to take no notice of my entrance were Hadassah's family. All except Nava, who had come to her feet, hand over her mouth. Uri hissed something at her and she sat down.

I managed to resist the urge to look back over my shoulder to see what was going on out in the hall. Instead, I walked straight to Hadassah and said, "Mind if I sit down?"

Nava let out a whimper.

To my surprise, Uri said to me, "It may not be safe here." At least, I thought he was talking to me. He didn't actually look up.

"It's okay," I said. I sank down onto the bench. "They're not coming in. I've got bodyguards."

I tried to laugh, but it came out like a snort through my nostrils, which only drew curious stares from Hadassah's cousins. Nava looked at me in horror.

Okay, just do it, I told myself, *before you mess the whole thing up.*

Heaving in a huge breath, I put the proposal to them. I tried to include Uri and the rest of them with my eyes, but it was easiest to look straight at Hadassah. At least I was familiar with her blank stare. When I was finished, Uri was already shaking his head. The cousins went back to their lunches. Only Hadassah was still watching me, the way she had that morning. I couldn't do anything but watch back, until she said, "Uri, I think we must do this."

He barked something back at her in Hebrew. She barked back without even flinching. Nava looked from one of them to the other like she was watching a sudden death tennis playoff.

Finally, Uri stood up and headed for a garbage can with his trash. Hadassah looked once again at me.

"I will ask my father. If he says no, there is nothing we can do. If he says yes, Uri and I, and our cousins, will be there." I caught a gleam in her dark eyes. It was the kind of spark that siblings reserve only for their rivalry. "We will see," she said.

I gave the door a triumphant shove and was already saying, "Am I good, or am I good?" as I stepped into the hall. But there wasn't a sign of Trent, Celeste, Joy Beth, or Stevie. The bell rang, the hall emptied, and I stood there with my victory fading on my lips.

What the Sam Hill? I thought. Several possible scenarios flipped through my mind as I did a stiff-legged fast walk toward the locker hall.

They'd chased the Rednecks off.

The Rednecks had chased THEM off.

They'd gotten into a brawl and both groups were now in Mr. Stennis's office receiving their suspensions.

The cops had arrived and—

Duffy! I said to myself. *Stop!*

As I elbowed my way into the hall, most of the crowd was headed the other way, which made me feel like a salmon swimming upstream. By the time I actually got to my locker, the place was deserted and the last bell was ringing. There was still not a trace of any of my FF's.

It was a good thing Mr. Frohm never came out of his office until the aid had taken the roll. I didn't need any tardies dragging my chemistry grade down.

I put myself into a higher gear, pushed through the door that led to the breezeway between the humanities and the science/math buildings— and there he was in the sudden glare of sunlight.

Wolf.

His mouth split open close to my face, the yellowed teeth bared. All I could think of was that his breath smelled just the way I'd thought it would—like stale cigarettes and rancid bacon grease.

I took a step backward and found myself against the door. He stepped with me.

"You a Jew lover?" he said.

I said nothing.

"I said, 'Are you a Jew lover?'"

Somehow the word "lover" didn't sound natural coming out from between those teeth. I bet his own mother never responded in love to him. So I did the only thing that came to mind, which was to respond in well-disguised fear.

"Get away from me," I said.

His eyes narrowed at my motionless jaw. "What's the matter with yer mouth? What are you, a freak?"

I took advantage of his instant of puzzlement to duck around him and make a run for the door at the other end of the breezeway.

"You just better watch yourself!" he called after me.

I wasn't sure, but as the door closed behind me, I thought I heard him spit.

All I could do for the next couple of minutes was lean against the wall and listen to my heart pound in my ears. As it slowed, so did my thoughts. There were fewer interior screams of "Are you crazy? Run for it, Duffy!" and more tight-toothed snarls at "I HATE THAT NASTY LITTLE PIECE OF SLIME'S GUTS!"

I felt like spitting, myself.

When I was finally able to break into a canter to get to the chemistry classroom, one thought was perfectly clear: I wasn't going to tell any of the others what had just happened. If I did, I knew all bets were off, and I had to see Wolf and his mangy little pack get theirs. I wasn't sure I had ever felt that kind of revulsion in my life.

But there was the question of whether to tell Mom and Dad. We'd come so far, the three of us, in our openness, so leaving things out felt like lying. But all I had to do was even give them a hint that I might be in some kind of physical danger and Dad would have me on house arrest. I was convinced Hadassah and I had the same father.

I thought about it off and on all afternoon, and I was no closer to a decision when I got home, so I escaped to my room, dragging the phone in there so I could call Pastor. If I had THAT kind of news to tell my parents, it might soften the real blow.

To say that Pastor Ennis was pleased with my announcement would be the understatement of the millennium. I actually thought he was going to cry.

"I knew you would come up with something fantastic," he said. "I think this can have a tremendous impact."

"It isn't for sure yet," I said. "The Dayans still have to get the okay from their parents. And then we have to make sure some kids other than us actually show up. It would be kind of embarrassing if they put this whole thing together for five people."

"Leave that to me. I'm going to put calls in to some of the other clergy in the area and see if I can't get them to bring their groups. We'll fill up the fellowship hall."

"Just let me make sure first—"

But I knew the minute we hung up he was going to break out the phone book. I couldn't help wondering what was going on over at Hadassah's right now.

I flopped back on my bed and closed my eyes. *I wonder if she's told HER father about the threats,* I thought. Of course, all he had to do was go up to the school and raise a stink and this whole thing would be over. Panama Beach was famous for catering to the rich people, and you didn't let your kids drive around in a Lincoln Navigator unless you had some bucks.

I rolled over and spotted my copy of The Message on the bedside table. Mrs. Isaacsen's Scriptures. The tug to read them was unmistakable.

She'd written three verses on the frog paper, and I thumbed for the first one.

"Here's another old saying that deserves a second look:," it said in Matthew 5:38-42. "'Eye for eye, tooth for tooth.' Is that going to get us anywhere? Here's what I propose: Don't hit back at all. If someone strikes you, stand there and take it. If someone drags you into court and sues for the shirt off your back, gift wrap your best coat and make a present of it. And if someone takes unfair advantage of you, use the occasion to practice the servant life. No more tit-for-tat stuff. Live generously."

I sank back into the pillows.

Am I doing that, God? If I'd slapped Wolf, or if I turn him in, that would be hitting back.

It was like Hadassah and her family were doing better at following the Jesus-words than I was.

I looked back at the Bible. *Use the occasion to practice the servant life.*

We were definitely doing that with the forum. My eyes closed, and I expected the peace that always came when I was on the same page with God. I even waited for a tug from the silken rope, pulling me on to the next thing.

But what I actually had was a strange halfway feeling, as if I were only partially right.

"What's up with this, Father?" I whispered. "All I want to do is what YOU want me to do. I'm doing it, aren't I?"

I pulled absently at my lower lip, which relieved the annoyance of having it crammed up against a mouth full of metal all day. There had to be more to it than the forum. After all, Wolf and Joe Philip and Quentin wouldn't be showing up there to get educated.

Unless I asked them.

I sat straight up in the bed. What would actually happen if I asked Wolf to come? THAT would be the servant thing to do, the generous thing, instead of telling my father he'd backed me up against a wall and threatened me. If I could stand talking to the scrawny little yellow-toothed slime ball. I got a nasty taste in my mouth.

Am I just asking for more trouble for the Dayans? I thought.

The only person who could really answer that question was Joy Beth. I looked at the clock radio. She was probably studying with Trent right now, and I didn't want to give her an excuse to lose focus. Her grades had improved about a thousand per cent since they'd been going out, but only because Trent MADE her do her homework with him every afternoon.

So I decided to wait until the next day. And I put off telling Mom and Dad, too, until after I had a chance to talk to her.

The whole evening, I avoided calling any of them, especially Celeste who would be able to read my mind right through the phone line. Strangely, none of them called me either. I still didn't know what had happened with Celeste's "Goon Squad," but it couldn't have been too bad, I decided, or I would have heard.

I got to my locker before anybody the next morning. When I opened it, a parchment envelope slid out, my name printed on it in letters no one else could make.

"It's about time you showed up," I said out loud.

I snatched up the envelope with shaking fingers and pressed it against my chest. *Please don't give me a riddle this time. Please tell me what to do.*

Struggling to get my backpack off, I sat down on it and let the envelope rest in my lap for a moment. God, please—he always seems to tell me what You want me to hear.

I picked it up and carefully slit the flap open with my fingernail. The paper was, as always, perfectly folded, but this time there was something tucked in with it, and it fell out into my open palm. It was a small, round mirror, about the size of a compact, and its beveled edges were framed with a narrow band of gold. It was so light and thin, I hadn't felt it through the envelope.

I shook out the paper with my other hand and read the few printed words.

You cannot yet love recklessly, the way the Father wants.
Look closely. Look within.
You must first wipe away the sneer on your face before you can wash the smudges from theirs.
Love and only love can take that away.
Your Secret Admirer

Leaning back against the lockers, I looked into the mirror. As small as it was, all I could see was one feature at a time. My eyes, looking confused, unclear. My nose, the nostrils flared—

Good grief! I thought. *You could drive the Dayan's' SUV through those!*

I was almost afraid to check out my mouth, and when I did, what I saw made me turn the mirror over and plaster it against my thigh with my hand. If lips pressed in until the chin grew hard and puckered didn't constitute a sneer, I wasn't sure what did.

I snatched up the note again. *You must first wipe away the sneer on your face before you can wash the smudges from theirs. Love and only love can take that away.*

"I don't get it," I whispered. "If I didn't love, I wouldn't be doing all this!"

I glanced in the mirror again. Okay, I had to get rid of THAT look in a HURRY.

I headed for the science wing. Joy Beth would be there, cloistered with Trent among the test tubes—he was an incurable romantic, that boy. All I had to know was whether I really needed to worry about being shut up in a freezer if I invited Wolf to the forum.

But they were all waiting for me at the end of a row of lockers—Celeste, Stevie, AND Joy Beth and Trent.

I don't want to talk to ALL of them, I thought. I let my steps slow as I waved to them. Man, I felt guilty.

But not half as guilty as they looked, once I got close enough to see Trent's eyes blinking everywhere but at me, and Joy Beth studying the toes of her Nikes, and Stevie examining the split ends she didn't have. Only Celeste was looking at me, and she cracked open like an egg the second I stopped beside her.

"Okay—so we ditched you yesterday," she said. "I know it was lame and we're all a bunch of losers but we were afraid if you found out what happened you'd change your mind."

"Am I supposed to know what you're talking about?" I said.

"No," Trent said. "I don't even know what she's talking about. I was the one who wanted to tell you right then."

"Tell me what?"

"But as usual, the women won," Stevie said.

I planted myself in front of Joy Beth. "You want to tell me what's going on?"

"It wasn't that easy keeping them dudes out of the courtyard while you were talking to that Hadassah chick," she said. She shrugged. "Didn't think it would be."

"Yeah, but did you think Celeste was going to have to make a date with one of them to keep them out of there?" Stevie said.

"YOU gave me the idea!" Celeste said. "The way you were acting, I thought that was what YOU were gonna do."

I could feel my eyeballs bulging from their sockets. "You're actually going to go OUT with one of them?" I said.

"I told you she'd hate it," Joy Beth said.

"No stinkin' way I'm gonna GO," Celeste said. "I just made him THINK I would."

She flipped around to Stevie—and for the first time I noticed Celeste was in black from headband to sandals. I was sure that as usual she was making some kind of statement, but she looked like somebody had just died. I was surprised she didn't have a veil over her face, for Pete's sake.

"Don't think I didn't see you flirting with Joe Philip to keep his eyes off that window," she said to Stevie.

"Uh, I do not BELIEVE so. I'd rather be shot, and he knew it." Stevie put her hand on Celeste's arm. "But I'm tellin' you, Sugar, Quentin thinks he's pickin' you up at eight."

"Tell me I'm not hearing this!" I said. I looked at Joy Beth. "I KNOW you didn't try to hook up with Wolf while all this was going on."

She grunted.

"Wolf took off," Trent said. He grinned proudly at Joy Beth. "I think she scared him."

"You guys did NOT have to go that far!" I said.

"It worked, didn't it?" Celeste said. "You asked Hadassah without being harassed."

It was my turn to look away. I glanced at my watch and headed for my locker. "So this is why nobody called me last night to find out what happened?" I said over my shoulder.

"We took a vow not to," Celeste said. "We knew we'd crack. Besides, it doesn't matter. She said yes, right?"

"We saw her nodding her head at you," Stevie said.

"Was that before or after you practically kissed Joe Philip on the cheek?" Celeste said.

"I did not ki—"

But Stevie was cut off in mid-word by a scream that curled up in terror from the bank of lockers across from hers.

"She's got a gun!" someone shouted above it. "Get down!"

As Celeste dove onto me and took me to the floor, I heard the popping sounds reverberating against the lockers.

chaptereight

Bedlam reigned as a chorus of terrified screams followed the shots. The crowd shoved its way out of control, several members of it stomping on my hand as they tried to join either the throng heading out, or the mob pressing in. Panic rose in my chest, and I scrambled to get out from under Celeste and up on my knees.

Between the bodies hurling themselves in frenzied directions, I was able to catch disjointed snatches of what was playing out across from us like scenes on MTV.

Nava staring at a huge gun, a hyperbole in her tiny hands.

Uri suddenly there, snatching it away from her.

Two Student Resource Officers materializing out of nowhere.

One ordering the crowd to move out—which no one did.

The other facing Uri and shouting, "Drop the gun, son."

The sound of metal hitting the floor.

As I got to my feet, voices exploded from the crowd that refused to budge.

"He shot it!"

"No, SHE did!"

"Anybody hurt?" the SRO barked above the din.

There was an abrupt silence as everyone looked at everyone else. In my own search, I saw that Joy Beth and Trent had Stevie plastered against the lockers, and she was peeking out from under Trent's armpit. The way he was sweating, that couldn't have been good.

"You hurt, Duffy?" Celeste whispered to me

I shook my head—just like everybody else, including those now rubber-necking from the tops of the lockers.

"All right people, let's move on out," one SRO called out in a drone. "There's nothing to see here."

A collective murmur of disappointment rippled through the crowd as they turned reluctantly to shuffle away. Mr. Stennis and Dr. Vaughn had arrived on the scene by now and were ripping people from the locker tops by backs of shirts and waistbands of jeans. The two S.R.O.s had Uri's hands pinned behind his back. The last glimpse I got before Celeste steered me around the corner was Nava crumpling into a dead faint. Two arms reached down for her, a ponytail swinging over one shoulder. I wanted to go back and see if it was Ponytail Boy—but the crowd was shoving us along and there was no turning around.

"She's fakin' it!" some kid near us said.

"Shut up," I said to him. "Just shut up."

But no one did. It was all anybody could talk about. They might as well have called off classes for all the teaching that got done. I think I heard every rendition of it in my first period MAPPS English class, even from the brightest kids.

One girl swung her pen around by the bent hook on its top and said, "What was that girl thinking, bringing a GUN to school?"

The kid leaning out the side of his desk, chewing open-mouthed on his gum, said, "Those kid's don't know about 'zero tolerance'— they're not from around here."

"Uh, ya think?" That came from a girl who took only that brief moment to look up from picking her nails to speak.

Pen-Girl switched to a rubber band for amusement. "She's sick of the guys harassing her in the halls."

"No, ya'll," said the boy who never stopped jiggling his heel, toe planted firmly on the floor. "It was the guy—he's the one that fired the shots."

Finally Mr. Brain Child, a sort of wide, dark-haired kid in the back with a baby face dotted in stubble and pimples, put in the final thought that was, as always, designed to bring the rest of us underlings to a screeching intellectual halt. "Those shots weren't from that gun. That was a 357 Magnum. He would've blown a hole in something with that thing."

Then he withdrew back into the posture that placed his tailbone at the front edge of the chair.

The girl who sat next to me stopped flipping the pages of *The Grapes of Wrath* against her cheek and looked at me. "I still say I heard shots," she whispered.

"They didn't come from Uri," I said—out loud. "And they sure didn't come from Nava."

"Then were did they come from?" Jiggle Boy said.

Suddenly the room was quiet, even though the bell had yet to ring. That was probably because I rarely joined in a discussion in that class. To them, I was still the New Kid—and I never liked the possibility that Brain Child would hurl some caustic come-back that it would take weeks for me to recover from. Besides, the jaw-wired thing made me sound like a moron. Nobody except the FF's could seem to get past that.

"I have no idea," I said. "But they're a peaceful family. They came here to get away from the violence."

Gum Guy twisted his lanky frame around to look at me. "You can't go anywhere to get away from violence. It's a fact of life."

I stared at him. "So you're just going to accept that?"

"What else am I supposed to do? Matter of fact, if I'm them, I'm armed all the time. You're an Arab, you walk in here with all these military brats whose relatives just fought the war in Iraq, you better expect some backlash."

"Hello!" I said. "They're not Arab—they're Israeli—"

"A raghead's a raghead," Jiggle Foot said.

"Gross generalization," Brain Child put in, then pulled back into his snail shell.

"That is SO—ignorant!" My cheeks were ablaze from the inside out. I strained against the wires to get my teeth apart. "Do YOU want people to assume you're inbred just because you come from the Panhandle?" I said to Jiggle Foot.

"He is inbred." The girl with the rubber band winked and shot it at him.

The bell rang, and Mrs. Wren strolled in already telling us to get out our character sketches of the Joad family.

"I want time left over to talk about 'Odyssey of the Mind'," she said. "So let's get started."

OM was a huge thing among the brightest-and-best at 'Nama High. They had won two states and a national championship in the past few years, and a new team was about to be picked. It was highly selective, and inclusion practically guaranteed a scholarship. Brain Child sat up in his seat and watched Mrs. Wren as if she were going to announce the members right then. While everyone else went into a buzz about it, Jiggle Boy poked Gum Guy and nodded toward me. "When did she get in this class?" he said.

I was still seething when I got to second period, ready to vent to Stevie. I barely had a chance to pry my lips open when Hadassah sat down next to us.

"Are you okay?" Stevie said to her.

Hadassah shook out her hair. "Before you start your interrogation—my family does not own guns. We do not know who put that weapon in Nava's locker."

"You think someone planted it in there?" I said.

"How could they? She has given the combination to no one."

"There are ways," Stevie said. "I used to hang out with a bunch of kids who did that kind of stuff all the time. What I want to know is, if it wasn't Uri's, how come he shot it?"

"He did not shoot it."

My eyes bulged. "Nava didn't shoot it, like—by accident?"

"No one shot it." Hadassah gave a disdainful sniff. "I heard the noise behind me as I was turning the corner. It came just as Nava pulled the gun from her locker."

"Somebody ELSE was shooting?" I said.

"They were not gunshots. I have heard those many times."

Stevie snapped her fingers. "Firecrackers! I KNEW that sound was familiar. But when somebody yelled 'She has a gun!' my mind went straight to bullets." She bumped her forehead with the heel of her hand.

Hadassah was nodding. "The Student Resource Officer found firecrackers on the floor just after Nava and Uri were taken to the office."

"Whew!" I said. "So—have they let them go yet? I mean, that's proof that this whole thing was a set-up."

"They have no proof that Nava did not place the gun in her locker herself. My father is here now."

"Then he'll get it straightened out," I said. "He's got a lot of—well, they'll listen to him."

"Will they?" Hadassah's face darkened, and her eyes darted up to Mr. Beecher.

He was standing at his podium, watching her as he tapped the eraser end of his pencil on his grade book.

"What's his issue?" Stevie whispered. "I never saw him get so intense about checking the roll before. Half the time he doesn't even do it."

"I have been receiving such looks all morning from teachers," Hadassah said. "Those who have simply ignored me before now treat me with suspicion."

"No stinkin' way!" I said. "They can't believe you guys were actually going to shoot up the school!"

"Does he not look as if he believes it?" Hadassah said.

I sneaked a peek at Mr. Beecher. His eyes were narrow and cool as he swept them over Hadassah one more time before turning to the chalkboard. I suddenly wanted to smack somebody, preferably him.

"That is just messed up," Stevie said.

Hadassah shrugged and opened her textbook, perching her glasses on the end of her nose. "Last night my father said yes to your request. I hope this does not mean he will change his mind."

"Won't he want you to do it more than ever?" Stevie said. "This could really make a difference in how kids treat you."

But her voice didn't have its usual lilt. If she was anything like me at that moment, she didn't feel much like celebrating.

By third period, in fact, I wanted somebody to pay, in a major way. If one more person said anything about Hadassah's family not being from around here or said 'Nama High was going to turn into another Columbine any second, I was afraid I was going to slug them with my backpack. I knew if I looked in my little mirror, my lip would be curled halfway up my nostrils.

When I got to Mrs. Isaacsen's for our group meeting, Celeste and Stevie were already there, and I dumped my backpack on the floor between them with a resounding thud.

"This youth forum thing has to be for REAL," I said. "I want it to stop all this stupid—STUPIDNESS!"

"Your neck veins are bulging, Duffy," K.J. said. "I used to get like that."

"I'd rather see you like that than the way you've been lately," Stevie said.

I slammed my hand down on Mrs. I.'s desk. "Is anybody even listening to me?"

"We are now," Celeste said.

Stevie peeled my hand off the desktop and rubbed it between hers. "Our forum is gon' be awesome—people will be blown away—"

"I don't mean just impress people. I want it to make a DIFFERENCE. I want it to make people stop acting like morons."

"You mean, like pulling a big ol' gun out of a locker and shooting it?"
I whipped my head around to see Michelle standing in the doorway.

"THAT'S what I'm talking about!" I said, jabbing my finger toward
her. "Nava didn't bring that gun, and Uri didn't fire it! And if anybody
knew a thing about the Dayans they'd never say something so—"

"Uninformed," Stevie said quickly. She squeezed my hand tight, but I
wrenched it away.

Michelle's eyes glittered at me before they glazed over. "Whatever,"
she said, and sat down in her usual seat.

"What's goin' on?" Joy Beth was now in the doorway, face taut
between panels of hair. "What's wrong, Duffy?"

"I'm hacked off," I said. "I HATE what's happening around here. It
was bad enough when the Dayans were being harassed, but now
somebody's trying to make it look like they're attacking back, and they're
NOT! Can't anybody see that?"

"So you think it was Wolf and them that set them up?" Celeste said.
Joy Beth snorted.

"What?" Stevie said to her.

"They aren't smart enough to think somethin' like that up."

"Oh, I don't know," K.J. said. She stretched up her neck so that her
big silver hoop earrings grazed her face. "Expecting people to think
firecrackers going off sounds like an assault weapon firing? That sounds
like about their speed. What I don't know is how they pulled it off when
they got suspended for a week yesterday. They aren't even here today."
K.J. jerked her chin at me. "But don't worry about it, Duffy. My old man
came down here himself. Your Jews are off the hook."

"They brought in the chief of police?" Celeste said. She gave a long
whistle.

"Only because I go here," K.J. said. "He's doing this big 'father of the
year' thing right now. He came down to make everybody think he's all
concerned about my safety."

K.J. spat out the last few syllables like they were drops of acid and
folded herself into the chair.

Stevie turned to me. "If it all got cleared up, then Hadassah's daddy
will probably still let them do the forum. Isn't that what we really want?
To get people to start understanding?"

"What I want is to find out if it was those creeps who planted that
gun," Celeste said.

"I think I like Stevie's approach much better."

At some point Mrs. Isaacsen had stepped in, and she now moved to stand behind Michelle's chair, the usually-feathery lines around her mouth deep and sharp. It was very un-Mrs. I.

"There is far more power in educating ourselves so that we can act with integrity," Mrs. Isaacsen said. "Much more power than in trying to make someone pay."

Celeste frowned. "So what do we do—let them get away with terrorizing people?"

"We let K.J.'s 'old man' take care of that part." Mrs. I. smiled at K.J. "No matter what his reasons are."

"Right," K.J. muttered. "It'll sound good for him in court."

"What does that mean?" Celeste said.

But as the bell rang for the period to start, K.J. glowered at her and Celeste said, "I guess we won't go there."

"But can we still talk about the forum?" Stevie said.

Mrs. I. nodded slowly. "I think it has a lot to do with what we're about in here—but the rules still apply."

"Yes, ma'am," Stevie said.

She got into her take-charge position—hair thrown back and face poised. It occurred to me that if she hadn't dumped the in-crowd, she might have been elected student body president for next year. She pulled both Celeste and me into the explanation and even got the occasional grunt out of Joy Beth.

When we were through, Mrs. I. said, "I'm impressed. That kind of exchange of ideas will give you power to effect change."

"Mmmm-hmmm."

We all looked at Michelle. This was the second time in thirty minutes that she'd joined in the conversation without having it pried out of her—and to challenge Mrs. I., no less. Even K.J. unfolded a little.

"What does THAT mean?" Celeste said.

Michelle shrugged. "Isn't it just talk?"

"We'll be informed," Stevie said. "Then we won't act out of ignorance."

"That's fine for the people who are there," Michelle said. "But what about everybody else?"

"What if everybody else is there?" I said. "Or at least a representative?"

Stevie stared at me. "What are you talking about?"

"What if I invite Wolf to the forum, and he comes?"

Joy Beth gave a loud, guttural grunt.

"You don't seriously think he'll come," Stevie said.

Celeste put her hands on her hips. "And you don't seriously think you'll ask him—not without an army standing behind you!"

I turned to Mrs. Isaacsen. "Isn't that what responding in love means? I can't keep walking around with this hate sneer on my face—but I can't let stuff like this keep happening either."

"But you also cannot set yourself up to be physically hurt," Mrs. Isaacsen said.

"Besides," K.J. said, "there's no way you're going to teach a bunch of jerks to love their neighbors."

The bell rang, and suddenly I wanted to be the first one to bolt out of there. My insides were shaking.

The next person who says a word to me is likely to get her nose plucked off, I thought.

"Laura?" Mrs. Isaacsen said. "Would you stay for a moment?"

I put my hand up to my mouth. *Dear God,* I prayed, *please tell me I didn't just say that out loud.*

But Mrs. Isaacsen didn't show signs of fearing for her nostrils, so I sat back down in the chair and waited for everybody else to file out. Mrs. Isaacsen closed the door behind them.

That can't be good, I thought.

She sat in a chair across from me, hands folded precisely in her lap like she wanted everything from then on to be orderly and clear.

"I like what you're doing with this church forum, Laura," she said. "I think it's an inspired idea."

I nodded a thanks. I was holding my breath.

"I just want to make sure you're doing it out of love, not out of anger."

"I AM angry! But I'm trying not to be. I'm trying to do what the verse said."

"I think you are, but—"

"You can still see the sneer on my face, right?" I could feel tears coming. "I don't want to be a hateful person—but I FEEL hate."

"So what do you do now?"

I looked at her blankly, blinking back the tears. "I thought I was doing it. I'm not hitting back. I'm doing the servant thing."

"And?"

I squirmed. "And what?"

"Did you read the rest of the passage, the other two verses?"

"Oh," I said. "No."

She reached inside a drawer and pulled out her Bible. "I think I need to read this out loud to you," she said.

I closed my eyes as she began to read.

"You're familiar with the old written law, 'Love your friend.' And its unwritten companion, 'Hate your enemy.' I'm challenging that. I'm telling you to love your enemies. Let them bring out the best in you, not the worst. When someone gives you a hard time, respond with the energies of prayer, for then you are working out of your true selves, your God-created selves."

My eyes sprang open. "You want me to pray for them?"

"GOD wants you to pray for them."

"But they're evil!" I said. "I've seen it—up close and personal. That Wolf person got right in my face—I could smell it on him. He's nothing BUT hate."

"All the more reason to put your energy into praying for him."

"But what good is it going to do? It isn't going to change him or any of them—unless there's a miracle or something."

Mrs. Isaacsen's eyebrows shot up. "Let me get this straight. You think YOU can change them by inviting them to your forum—but you don't think GOD can change them no matter what."

I couldn't answer her.

"We don't know if your prayers will be the thing that changes these boys," Mrs. Isaacsen said. "But we do know that it will change you." She fingered the keys on my bracelet and then sat back in her chair.

"So I have to pray for them," I said. "Even if I don't want to."

"We'll let God work on the wanting part. You just get down on your knees."

Even though it was end-of-April warm, I hugged my arms around myself as I hurried toward the courtyard.

What just happened? I thought.

Because something had—and now I had to move in a whole new direction.

For the rest of the day, I couldn't get my mind off of having to pray for people I absolutely detested. Everybody kept asking me what was wrong, but I couldn't put it into words yet. Besides, I was too busy badgering God.

Do I really have to do this? Lord, please! How am I supposed to say, "Please bless Wolf and Quentin and Joe Philip? Hold them in your everlasting arms?. And please fill Mr. Beecher and the other prejudiced teachers with your love—and all the kids who just stand around waiting for a good fight". How can I do that, God?

In His usual fashion, God didn't answer me right away. Where was that speed dial when you needed it?

I was still so engrossed in it on the way home that afternoon—that and listening to Jami Smith tell me His love was deep and high and long and wide and in all ways bigger than anything I could possibly produce, or, at least the way I looked at it—that I jumped when the buzzer on my gas gage told me, obnoxiously, that I needed fuel. I pulled into a Citgo and dug around in my backpack for my gas money. When I turned to open my door, there was somebody staring at me through the window.

It was a scrawny, greasy-haired boy with yellow teeth. He had a mouth like a Wolf.

chapter**nine**

"Dear God," I whispered. It was the only praying I could do at the moment.

There were too many voices in my head, from Mrs. Isaacsen to Owen, telling me to get OUT of there.

But Wolf yanked the door open and squatted down beside me, one hand on each side of my doorway. I was sure that from the outside, it looked like a cozy little boy-girl thing.

Please, God, please—

What was I supposed to be doing? Praying for escape, or praying for HIM? All I could actually form in my mind was, God, please do your thing in this kid.

"I told you to watch it," he said.

I shrank back from the rancid breath, but I kept my eyes on his. "Does that mean I can't stop for gas?"

"It means you better watch what side you take."

"I'm not taking sides. You are."

I wasn't sure where the words were coming from, but wherever it was, it wasn't making Wolf happy. He actually bared his teeth at me.

"If you aren't on my side, you're on the WRONG side."

"I'm on God's side," I said. I turned to the side to try to get out. "I need to get some gas."

I wasn't surprised that he didn't budge. I WAS surprised that he said, "That's right. God's side. Not the Jews' side."

I stared at him. Even the word God sounded obscene coming out of his mouth. What was I supposed to pray about that? God, please let his tongue fall out?

"I believe in God," Wolf said. "And I believe anybody that don't oughta be run outa town."

"You think you're doing this for God?" I said.

For an answer, he fished a toothpick out of his pocket and went after his incisors. I thought I would barf.

But instead, I saw my chance. It was part of an irresistible tug—and since I wasn't feeling much of that lately, I let it pull the words right out of my tightly-closed mouth.

"Okay," I said, "since you're into God—why don't you come to my church Wednesday night? We're having a forum about what the Jews believe and what we believe—about God. The Jewish kids are going to be there—they're the speakers."

Wolf yanked the toothpick out of his mouth, and for a few seconds I thought he was going to drag me from the car. I forced myself to stay perfectly still, until he drew his mouth into an ugly line and said, "Where's it gonna be?"

"Cove Community Church. Six thirty."

"Thank you," he said. "You just made my day."

With that he climbed into the unpainted truck with the oversized wheels and pealed out. From the side of the building, a Harley emerged, its driver wearing a helmet that hid his face behind tinted plastic. The ends of a ponytail blew out from under it.

Could that be—?

But I had a bigger question to consider: *Was that right, God?*

It must have been, I decided, because I was still in one piece.

Mentioning it to my parents was actually not an option, because when I got home, all they could talk about was the gun incident at school. The TV news already had Mom polishing the doorknobs. She always cleaned when she was about to go nuts worrying. The radio alerted Dad on his way home from work, raising his blood pressure into stroke range, I was sure. Even Bonnie greeted me at the door with, "Did you see that girl get shot, Laurie?"

"NO one got shot!" Mama said. Then she turned to me, wide-eyed, and added, "Did they?"

"Everybody needs to calm down," Dad said.

But at cereal time, it was the main topic of conversation between the two of us.

"I guess it's ridiculous to ask if you're still bent on going on with your program at the church," he said.

"We are," I said. I stopped with Big Bird's syringe halfway to my mouth. "You're not going to tell me not to, are you?"

Dad dumped a soupspoon full of brown sugar into his bowl. "I'm concerned. You're publicly aligning yourself with the people who are being attacked. That could make you a target too."

I felt a flicker of guilt, but I couldn't get out the words, 'I already AM a target.'

"We're doing it in the church," I said. "Who knows, maybe the attackers will even come."

Dad lifted an eyebrow.

"They've been invited."

"Oh, wonderful." Dad looked at me through the steam that curled up from his spoon. "There's only one way you are doing this forum, Laura—and that's if I come, too. Do we have a deal?"

"Sure," I said.

I was too surprised to say any more than that.

But I WAS tired of negotiating with people, so I wrote Owen an email instead of an IM. I had barely clicked SEND before the phone rang. I snatched it up, one eye on the doorway. If I let it ring again there was sure to be a parent arriving there momentarily, wanting to know why there was a call coming in at this hour.

"You really think having your dad there is going to mean nothing is gonna happen to you?" Owen said, in lieu of hello.

I let out a long, slow breath. Finally I was hearing Owen's voice—but this wasn't what I'd had in mind for our first phone call in weeks.

"Look, Laura," he said, "you know you're a magnet for losers with power issues. Next thing you know, they're gonna find your body washed up on the shore of St. Andrew's Bay."

"O-wen!" My voice screeched. I'm sure that wasn't what he'd had in mind, either.

There was a strained silence.

"Okay, look," he said finally. "Just promise me that you'll watch your back."

I sighed. "I wish you were here to watch it for me."

"I don't know if I could watch this," he said.

When we hung up, I had an ache right in the middle of my chest.

I went to my bedroom and unzipped my backpack. As always, there was still homework to do. As I pulled out my copy of *The Grapes of Wrath* the S.A.'s note came with it. The tug was strong to look in the mirror again.

I didn't want to. I knew what I was going to see. The sneer would still be there—even though I was at least trying to pray.

But when I actually looked, I gasped, right out loud. The sneer was there all right—and for a moment it looked just like the ugly gash that had formed on Wolf's lips that afternoon.

You must first wipe away the sneer on your face, the Secret Admirer had written to me, *before you can wash the smudges from theirs.*

Love and only love can take that away.

Love.

I squeezed my eyes shut, remembering.

Love your enemies.

Let them bring out the best in you, not the worst.

How?

Respond with the energies of prayer.

Why?

Then you are working out of your God-created self.

"Then that's what I have to do," I said out loud. "That's what we all have to do."

I gathered the FF's the next morning in the physics lab, where it was usually a safe bet nobody else would be there. Uri was, but when we all came in, he got up and left.

"I'm not so sure about this forum thing," Trent said when Uri was gone.

"We don't have to be," I said. "All we have to do is pray."

"Of course we're praying, Honey," Stevie said. "And the forum is going to be incredible. Did I tell you one of the churches is bringing a worship team—guitars and drums, the whole thing? I think that's going to be better than the ice breakers, I mean, you know, with the topic we've picked."

"I think it picked us," Celeste said. She was watching me closely. "But you're not just talking about praying for the forum, are you, Duffy?"

I shook my head. When I told them what I did mean, nobody would look at me.

"I know it's hard," I said. "I don't even know if I'm doing it right—mostly I'm just talking to God about them. Okay, arguing with Him."

"So we're not supposed to do anything BESIDES pray?" Celeste said. I didn't like the evasive look in her eyes.

"No," I said. "Celeste—did you do something already?"

"I tried. It didn't work."

"TELL me you didn't go out with—"

"I didn't exactly go out with him—I just hung out with him for a couple hours last night."

"Where?"

She cringed. "You don't want to know."

"Cel-E-este!" I said.

"Don't worry about it, Duffy. It didn't work anyway. All I got out of him was that it wasn't their idea to put the gun in Nava's locker—that it was somebody else's. But the firecrackers WERE his idea. He was all proud of that."

"I don't get it," Joy Beth said.

"I'm still getting over you actually hanging around that creep!" Stevie said to Celeste.

"'Somebody else' who?" I said.

"Whoever they're working with," Celeste said.

"There's more of them?" Trent said. He looked at Joy Beth. "How many relatives do you have?"

Celeste shook her head, blonde ponytail bouncing. "I would have had to do a lot more than just hang out with him to get that information."

"Well, thank goodness you had SOME sense," Stevie said.

"Hey, I took a hit for the team!" Celeste said.

"NO more hits!"

They all stopped and looked at me.

"We're supposed to let them bring out the best in us, not the worst," I said.

"I pretty much thought I WAS giving it my best!"

"It's not funny, Celeste."

There was a funky silence. I looked around.

"What's going on?" I said.

They avoided my eyes.

"Trent?" I said.

"All I did was do some research on the odds of being able to figure out somebody's locker combination by trial and error." He shook his unkempt head. "Practically impossible. You'd either have to get the combination or have some kind of device."

"I KNOW they don't got nothin' like that," Joy Beth said.

I squinted my eyes at her. "HOW do you know?"

She shrugged.

"Joy BETH…"

"I did some lookin' over at the place where they're all stayin'. I found out from my uncle."

"You went OVER there?"

"Me and my brothers—and Trent."

My eyes were practically popping from my head, I knew it.

"So you didn't find anything?" Celeste said.

Both Joy Beth and Trent shook their heads.

"So you all knew about this except me?" I said.

"Not me!" Stevie said.

Celeste folded her arms. "Don't act so innocent, Stevie. Tell her what YOU were doing."

I turned my eyes on Stevie, who was suddenly studying her cuticles.

"At least I didn't do anything dangerous," she said.

Joy Beth grunted.

"WHAT?" I said. It screeched out of me at the peak of frustration.

"I just went to the beach yesterday afternoon with some people who used to be my friends," Stevie said. "Just to see if they knew anything."

"And did you have to pretend to be their friends again?" Celeste said.

"That isn't the point! The point is—they have their own hate thing going against Hadassah and them."

"Who?" I said.

"Just a bunch of cut throats. They wouldn't give me any details, but they seem to be threatened by the Dayans and how intelligent they are."

"I bet every one of them has an I.Q. over 140," Trent said.

"That's all they told you?" Celeste said.

Stevie nodded. "They were still pretty suspicious of me. I had to work hard to get that much."

I would have given anything about then to have been able to chew my nails.

"Look—we were just trying to get more information, Duffy," Celeste said.

"And what were you going to do with it?"

"We—and you—" Stevie swept her eyes over the group. "We were going to take it to K.J.'s father. He would see justice done—you heard what K.J. said about him wanting to be Super-Dad."

"And if information does come our way, without us digging for it," Celeste said, "I think we should still do that. We have an in with the Chief of Police. Isn't that part of protecting the Dayans?"

"That's really going to get us in good with K.J.," I said. "She doesn't WANT her father involved."

"You could talk to her," Celeste said. "Everybody listens to you, Duffy."

In fact, they were listening now. Nobody said a word until I finally said, "Okay—yeah. But no more looking for dirt, okay?"

"Tell me why again?" Celeste said.

"Because it didn't bring out the best in us. You and Stevie both had to be fakes. Joy Beth and Trent had to go skulking around like spies."

"So you just want us to pray," Trent said.

"That's what I'm getting from God," I said.

"If Duffy says it's God, I'm in," Celeste said. "Besides, it'll make her life a lot easier. And mine. I got two emails from Owen last night."

"You, too?" Stevie said. "He's about having a breakdown thinking you're going to wind up in the morgue, Duff."

"Then, the Lord be with you," Celeste said.

"And also with you," Stevie said.

They all looked at me.

"Let us pray," I said.

We prayed until the bell rang for first period. Everybody was covered, even Wolf. It was hard. The best any of us could come up with for him was for some decent dental work. I figured it was something. We split up to go to class vowing that if we got the urge to do anything stupid, we'd just pray.

I'd no sooner walked in the door of first period than that little band of bright kids had me surrounded, as if they'd suddenly decided I existed. All except Brain Child, who sat on his spine in the corner, fiddling with a calculator. And even he had to glance quickly down at it every time I looked his way, maintaining his façade of indifference.

"You're friends with Stevie Martinez, right?" Pen Girl said.

"Yeah," I said.

"She and I used to be close, until she got religion. No offense, but she was more fun before."

I wanted to say, You mean, back when she used to pretend her friends didn't bully people and call it popularity? But I just made my way to my desk with all of them in tow. This had to be the result of Stevie's attempt at investigative work the night before.

Gum Guy parked himself on my desktop as if I'd invited him. "So—you hang out with that Israeli girl. Do you know what that whole gun thing was about?"

"If I knew who did it, I would have turned them in."

"No way!" Pen Girl. She picked up the pencil I'd just pulled out of my backpack. I reached up and took it back from her.

"Yes—way," I said.

"You won't see me setting myself up like that," said Jiggle Foot. He spread out his fingers to count on them. "There's been a fight in the cafeteria—graffiti on the front of the school—a gun in somebody's locker. I don't need that kind of damage."

"You missed the bottle somebody threw at their car in front of Books-a-Million," I said. "But nobody's asking you to put yourself out there."

Pen Girl took a Sharpie out of Gum Guy's pocket and took the cap off to smell the tip. "You're doing it, though," she said. "What's the deal?"

"Because it's the right thing to do," I said. "I hate prejudice and I'm trying to do something about it."

They all looked at me oddly for a minute. Then Gum Guy said, "I gotta ask—your mouth—"

The girl sitting next to me smacked him on the thigh. "That's so rude!"

But I shook my head and smiled at him so he'd get a full view of my wires. "This is what happened the last time I did the right thing. If I lived through that, I can live through anything."

I hadn't really put that together before, but the sound of it squeezing its way out between my teeth made me sit up straighter in the seat and look them all more directly in the eye until the bell rang. They went to their seats, giving each other I-can't-wait-to-put-this-chick-through-the-rumor-mill looks as they went. All except Brain Child, who watched me from his seat in the corner like he was calculating something in his head.

Probably figuring out the odds on whether I'll be killed or just scarred for life, I thought.

As I opened *The Grapes of Wrath*, I saw Pen Girl turn around in her seat and whisper hoarsely back at him.

"Hey, Daniel," she said, "you were right."

"Of course I was," he said. "About what?"

Pen Girl glanced back at Mrs. Wren, who was answering somebody's question, and scooted back to the corner to crouch by Daniel's desk. She was doing the Celeste style of whispering, so I could still hear her.

"I saw the application files in Mrs. Isaacsen's office," she said. "FOUR of those kids applied for OM."

"So?" Daniel said. But out of the corner of my eye I could see him sliding up further in the chair.

"So—they're totally smart. They speak, like, four languages."

"What—are we doing the project in Swahili? I'm not worried about it."

"Whatever," Pen Girl said. "But I counted fourteen applications."

She slid back into her desk just as Mrs. Wren looked her way. I sneaked another glance back at Daniel, the Brain Child. He was poking his finger at the keys of his calculator like they were ants he was trying to smash.

Were they talking about Hadassah and them? I thought. They had to be. Who else in this school speaks four languages?

Besides—the sneer in Pen Girl's voice had been unmistakable when she'd said "those kids."

How am I supposed to "respond in love" to that? I thought. HIS love might be deep and high, but mine was grounded in who deserved it.

The flames lapped at my cheeks. This fight was going to have to be fought on more levels than I'd thought. Basically, I wanted to scream at just about every kid in the room.

The announcements had started and, as usual, no one was listening, until Mr. Stennis's voice came over the intercom—reminding students that no weapons were allowed on campus, not even for use in practical jokes.

"That was SO not a joke," I said.

"I don't get you," Gum Guy said to me. "You don't open your mouth for three months and suddenly you're Diane Sawyer. You didn't talk this much BEFORE you got wired shut."

"Let's get back to *The Grapes of Wrath*," Mrs. Wren said.

"When are you going to announce who's in OM?" Brain Child said.

"Friday, Daniel," Mrs. Wren said. "And if you don't stop asking me about it, I may hold out even longer."

I managed to get through the rest of the day without going off on anybody. I started to actually calm down some when Hadassah surprised us by joining our table at lunch. She brought Nava with her, but the little freshman didn't say a word, or even look at any of us. Their brother and cousins did plenty of stony looking from across the courtyard.

"They don't want you guys sitting with us, do they?" Celeste whispered to Hadassah.

"They think we will bring more trouble on you," Hadassah said.

I glanced quickly at Trent, who stared down at his baloney sandwich. I was proud of him for not saying, "I think they're right!"

"I don't see how you could," Stevie said. "The Wolf Boys haven't been out here in days."

"They haven't even been in school," Joy Beth said.

"It does not matter," Hadassah said. "If you are willing to stand by us, then we must also stand by you."

All of us stared at her. Celeste was, of course, the first to break the silence with, "Well, that rocks."

In spite of the fact that the administration was calling the gun incident a practical joke, over the next few days, three more very scary-looking SRO's appeared on campus, and every outside door was either manned with one of them or kept locked.

"I feel like I'm coming into a penitentiary every time I walk in here," Trent said the morning of the forum.

We were standing in the hallway outside the locker area, working out some last minute details.

"It's always felt like Sing Sing to me," Celeste said, voice bright. "I figure it's just double protection for Hadassah and them."

"Or more of a challenge for the RM's."

I felt a pang of guilt. It was the first time I'd really remembered that I had invited the Redneck Militia to the forum. I had actually been too busy getting it ready. And praying for them.

"I have to get to class," I said.

I was about to walk into first period when Mrs. Isaacsen stopped me in the hall.

"I thought of something I wanted to tell you," she said. "Did you realize that Mr. Howitch is Jewish?"

I shook my head.

"You might want to talk to him, just to get more information."

"Okay," I said.

Then we both stood there, like she was expecting me to say more.

"I'm praying, Mrs. I.—for all my enemies. I never knew I had so many."

"I told you it would change you," she said.

"I'm not sure it has."

"Looked in a mirror lately?" she said.

I almost jumped out of my skin. It freaked me out whenever what she said lined right up with what the Secret Admirer said. There was a time when I'd even thought she was him.

As soon as I got to class, I took out the mirror. I wasn't sneering. Maybe this was working after all.

That was why I told Stevie to let everybody know I was going to see Mr. Howitch at the beginning of lunch. If praying and understanding WERE working, I had to do more of both.

He was perched on his stool in front of his music stand in the chorus room, eating a cheese sandwich with one hand and marking on *The Crucible* with the other. He looked so intent, I almost left without saying anything. Besides, I started to wonder exactly what I was going to say. How did you broach a subject like that? "Hey, Mr. H., I hear you're a Jew"?

I was actually about to step out when he looked up and motioned me in with the sandwich, Provolone flopping out the sides of the bread.

"Hey, Laura-Lou!" he said. "Come on in. I know why you're here."

"You do?" I said.

"Mrs. I. and I had lunch together yesterday." He put the sandwich on the music stand with the script and nodded for me to pull up a stool.

"She told me about your forum. I think it's an excellent idea. How can I help?"

"I don't know," I said. "We're all set up, and Hadassah's going to speak and then people will ask questions—I hope."

"Not to worry," Mr. H. said. "I think Hadassah will be pretty provocative."

I could feel my eyebrows going up. "You know her?"

"She goes to my synagogue." He pulled lightly at his nose. "Let's just say she isn't afraid to speak her mind."

"Yeah, but in front of a bunch of Christians? And after what's been happening to them here?"

Mr. H. swiveled around to face me. "There is no doubt in my mind that you and your group will make her feel like she has plenty of support."

"I'm praying for her," I said. Then I wanted to bite my tongue off. Was it okay to talk to a Jewish person about praying?

Good grief, I thought. *I'm still as ignorant as anybody else about all this!*

Suddenly, I blurted again. "I know it's short notice, but do you think you could come tonight? To the forum? I mean, unless you'd feel weird coming into the church—I mean a Christian church—I know you go to church, just not a—"

He was pushing his nose down against his moustache with his fingers. I had a feeling it was to cover the smile that was twitching on his lips.

"I'd be honored," he said. "I'll check my schedule."

I nodded. I was still nodding when the door opened and K.J. came in. Her eyes were focused on Mr. H. from the time the door closed behind her until she was right in front of him. I wasn't sure she even knew I was there.

"I can't be at rehearsal today," she said to him. "If you have to kick me out of the play, I'll understand."

I glanced at Mr. H., who was running his index finger back and forth under his nose. It was Howitch for, What are you TALKING about, child?

Instead he said, "I need a little more information."

"It's my old —my father," she said. Her voice was steady, almost dull, but her eyes were darting all over the place, advertising anxiety. "He just sprang something on me."

"You need me to talk to him?" Mr. H. said.

"It won't help. He can't change it. I told him you drop people if they have an unexcused absence but he doesn't care. All he cares about is winning."

Mr. Howitch glanced at me, and after a moment of cluelessness, I hopped off the stool and said, "I better go."

"She can stay," K.J. said. "My father made an appointment for me to meet with the lawyer so they can tell me what to say in court."

Mr. Howitch was nodding slowly, pulling at his nose. "If it's a legal matter, K.J., I can excuse you for that. But I'd like to talk to him."

I didn't have to look at K.J. to know she was stiffening. He didn't miss it either.

"It isn't that I don't trust you. I just need to know if he foresees any more unexpected appointments. As we get closer to performance, the rehearsals are going to be more and more important."

"Then you might as well just dump me right now," K.J. said. Her eyes went to slits. "Because he's the MAN—he knows all—he controls all."

With that, she raked her fingers through her hair and stormed out. Mr. Howitch gazed after her, the skin between his eyebrows pinched. I had no idea what to do.

"You mind going after her—maybe calming her down some?" he said.

I jerked around, hand to chest. "Me?"

Like there was anybody else in the room. I grabbed my backpack and made for the door. With any luck K.J. would be long gone. What the Sam Hill was I going to say to her?

Luck had not exactly been my constant companion lately. She was right outside the door, leaning against the wall. Her eyes still looked like sharp dashes as she stared at the ceiling. I could have felt her frustration from a hundred yards.

"You okay?" I said. "Stupid question—sorry."

"Why should you be sorry, Duffy?" she said. Her voice was pulled back like a stretched-out bungee cord. "How would you know? The word divorce isn't in your family's vocabulary."

"Oh," I said. "So your folks are splitting up?"

"Ripping up, is more like it." K.J. gave a bitter smile. "It's not them breaking up that gets to me. At least now I won't have to listen to them scream at each other every hour of the night."

"That bad, huh?"

"Worse. Don't even take me there. And the WORST is, they're putting me right in the middle of it."

"They're fighting over you?" I said. My hand clapped over my mouth. "I'm sorry! I didn't mean to make it sound like, 'Who would fight over YOU?'"

"No, man, I wish they DID feel that way. I love my mom, but she's a drunk and she won't even admit it when she wakes up in some dive down at the beach with her head on the bar. And my father is a control freak and he's afraid if he lets me out of the house for ten seconds I'm going to become an alcoholic just like her. Except for play rehearsals, I'm under freakin' surveillance all the time. I'm surprised my old man doesn't put an ankle bracelet on me so he can track me going from class to class."

"That's really—"

"I know what it is, Duffy, okay—it's the—" She formed a word on her lips and then bit it back. "I keep forgetting how religious you are. It's the pits—squared, okay? The thing is, if I don't choose one of them, the judge'll put me in foster care 'till I'm eighteen. I don't think so." K.J. rolled her eyes. "So today my father is dragging me to his lawyer so he can coach me on what to say in court about my mother that will keep her from getting custody of me. Like I don't already know. He's pushing me over the edge."

"Don't go there, K.J.," I said.

"I know. The play is the only thing that's keeping me sane. When I'm on stage, I can just be Mary Warren and all my stuff goes away and I replace it with hers."

I could see how that could help. Deciding between parents was a lot less monumental than deciding whether to let innocent people hang or be hanged yourself.

"Not only that," she said, "but if I get into any trouble at all, the judge will decide FOR me—and you know who he's going to put me with—his buddy, the Chief of Police." K.J. looked squarely at me. "Wonder what he'd say if I told him how many times the Chief has slapped me across the face?"

All I could do was shake my head.

"Don't worry about it, Duffy," she said.

As she walked away, my stomach turned over. If we turned information over to K.J.'s father that would make him the hero who rid his daughter's school of hate crimes, it might mean the judge would be more inclined than ever to stick K.J. with him—and if Chief O'Toole really did hit K.J. on a regular basis—

How could I NOT worry?

chapterten

I was still gearing up to tell the FF's that K.J.'s father had to be out of the picture when the five of us pulled into the church parking lot in Stevie's Expedition. There wasn't a single car there except Pastor's van. Another worry blotted out the first one.

"Nobody's coming," I said. "All this work—"

"Duffy, would you chill?" Celeste said. "We're two hours early. Were you expecting people standing in line for the doors to open?"

"Oh," I said. "I'm a little stressed."

"You think?" Stevie said. She threw an arm around my shoulders as we walked across the parking lot loaded up with grocery bags. "You didn't say a word all the way here. What's going on?"

I decided then that we should talk about it later. My poor brain could only pray about one thing at a time.

God, please, just open up people's minds. Please. And get them here...

Trent and Joy Beth got busy setting up for the panel while Stevie organized her notes and Celeste and I worked in the kitchen getting the food ready. There wasn't much to it, since my mother had given me a list of what chips should go in what baskets and notes on how to display her array of cookies on the platters.

"As if any kid is going to care what they look like on the plate," I said to Celeste. "And who's gonna eat this rabbit food? What do you want to bet most of these carrots will be left over?"

But she shook her head. "Mama Duffy always makes everything a class act," she said. "And not everybody is a slob."

"I guess not," I said. "Otherwise, why would we even be doing this?"

"We WOULDN'T be doing this if it weren't for your dad," Trent said from the doorway. "We can't get the lights to work—but he thinks he can fix them."

"He got here?" I said.

"Yeah, but he went home to get a ladder. And get this—Uri let him use his Navigator to go pick it up."

"The Dayans are here already?" Celeste said.

I looked forlornly at the huge spread of food. "Well, at least there will be somebody to eat all this stuff. I feel like Pastor Ennis with the pizza."

"Why?" Trent said. "There's already 150 kids out there doing ice breakers with Stevie. Who knew they'd all get here a half hour early?"

"No stinkin' way!" Celeste and I said together.

"Stinkin' way," Trent said. "As soon as your dad gets the lights fixed, we're starting."

Celeste looked me. Even her freckles were dancing. "Oh, ye of little faith," she said.

"Thank you, God," I said.

That was one prayer answered. But still, after all the times I'd been in front of an audience singing, I'd never been as nervous as I was when we walked into the fellowship hall and saw what looked like about a THOUSAND kids packed in there. There were two guys with guitars and a girl with a keyboard leading the crowd in "Open the Eyes of My Heart, Lord." Pastor was standing in the back with my dad and a couple of other adults who had to be ministers, judging from the I-am-so PROUD-of-these-young'uns looks on their faces. Dad grinned at me.

I had to grin back, mostly because he didn't appear to be looking for snipers. He actually looked like he wanted to shout, "This was MY Baby Girl's idea!" Thank the ever lovin' Lord he didn't.

Besides, who would have heard him? The din was louder than the halls at school—until the song was over and Stevie stepped up to the microphone and said, "Hey, ya'll!"

There was a unanimous reply of "Hey, ya'll,"—some of it in the voices of posturing males trying to imitate her.

And then a hush fell, as Hadassah, and Uri, and Nava, and all their cousins, filed in from the side door and took their places at the panel under 150 silent stares. The only thing that kept me from shouting,

"Okay—forget it—this is never going to work!" was the sight of Mr. Howitch following them in and sitting at the end of the front row.

Was he praying with them back there? I wondered. *Do they do that, like we do?*

I wasn't sure I was as relieved to see four Middle-Eastern men with beanies in the back row. Although Pastor slid in beside them, smiling, their faces remained expressionless.

"Those are some scary looking dudes," Celeste whispered to me.

The worship leader—a tall kid in baggy shorts—led the crowd in prayer. I didn't peek to see how Hadassah was reacting, though when I opened my eyes at the amen, she still had hers closed.

"We're going to start by having Hadassah speak," Stevie was saying, "and then ya'll can ask questions and whoever up here on the panel wants to answer can. We hope ya'll have some questions prepared."

I saw a couple of people put pieces of paper briefly up in the air.

Hadassah stepped up to the podium and looked out over the crowd. She was wearing her hair straight and brushed back over her shoulders, and it shone in the lights like liquid dark chocolate. She had her glasses in hand, poised at the edge of the podium, and her black eyes below the strong brows looked straight into the eyes of the people who gaped back at her as if she were some specimen they'd never viewed before.

When she started to speak, I knew she was unfazed by that. Her voice was deep and steady as she said, "We are all creations of God. We are all loved by God. If we believe that, there is hope for understanding here tonight." She raised her hand slowly into the air and once again her eyes swept over the audience. "I, for one, believe that. Do you?"

There was an uncertain silence.

Standing along the side of the audience, I put my hand up. So did Celeste—and Joy Beth—and Stevie. Even Trent. The adults all waited as if they were taking one unanimous inhale.

I squeezed my eyes shut. *God, please! Please make them understand.*

There was a hum in the room, and Hadassah spoke again.

"Yes," she said. "There is hope."

I opened my eyes. Every hand was in the air.

After that, it couldn't have been any cooler.

Hadassah talked about how Jesus was a Jew, and how he loved his people and used their Scriptures to teach them. People really seemed to start getting it when she had Uri and Drool Boy, from our own youth group, stand up, and had the audience figure out which one looked more like what Jesus probably looked like, given where he was born. Uri, of course, won by a landslide.

"She is so stinkin' good at this," Celeste whispered to me.

She really was. When she got to her closing, I didn't want her to stop.

"One of your greatest evangelists," she said, "the Reverend Billy Graham, has said that many who claim to be Christians could not possibly be true Christians in the biblical sense. If a professing Christian is not living his life out of love for his neighbor, he cannot be called Christian. Many of the persecutors of the Jews have been false Christians who dragged the name of Jesus through the mud of prejudice." She paused and for the last time scanned the crowd with her intense brown eyes. "I beg you to be true to the teachings of your Master Jesus."

People were on their feet whistling and clapping for so long, Pastor finally had to help Stevie shout them down so we could go on to questions. I sagged happily against the wall—until about halfway through the Q&A.

A guy raised his hand and, when Stevie called on him, he stood up. Celeste about broke one of my ribs poking me in the side.

"That's Richard!" she said in what was supposed to be a whisper.

Like I hadn't known it from the minute he smiled at Hadassah. He was the first boy I'd ever had a crush on, so there was no forgetting the long legs, the hair tousled over the forehead, the lazy touch of a Florida Panhandle accent.

"Your speech was awesome," he said to Hadassah. "I learned a bunch of stuff I didn't know before, didn't ya'll?"

I found myself nodding along with everybody else. I had to admit that Richard was one of the nicest guys on the entire planet, even if he HAD dumped me without giving me a chance to redeem myself. I remembered that he was always doing the whole encouraging thing, and was actually sincere about it. I noticed now that he'd gotten his braces off since the last time I'd seen him. Dang it, he was cuter than ever.

"Let me just get straight on this one thing, though," Richard said. "You don't believe that Jesus is the Savior."

"We believe that he was a great teacher," Hadassah said, "and that he changed the world to be a better place in many ways."

"But you don't believe that by believing in Him and following Him, you'll have eternal life."

Uri took the microphone from his sister. "No," he said. "Your Jesus is not our Messiah."

"Okay," Richard said. He ran a hand up and down the other muscular arm.

I found myself wishing he'd sit down.

"So let me ask you this," he said. "Why DON'T you believe it?"

"Uh-oh," Joy Beth said under her breath.

It's okay, I thought. *We're supposed to be exchanging ideas.*

But I couldn't help glancing nervously at Hadassah's father and uncles in the back row. They sat unnaturally still, their eyes riveted to Uri. In the front row, Mr. Howitch was pulling on his nose.

"Because the Messiah is yet to come," Uri said.

"Okay," Richard said. "So that's why the Jews killed Jesus, because they thought he was a fake?"

The back row looked as if rigor mortis had set in. Uri looked at one of them, his face as expressionless as all of theirs, but something apparently passed between them, because he looked back at Richard and spoke in an even voice.

"The situation for the Jews under Roman rule was so dangerous at that time," Uri said, "that the very survival of the Jewish people was at stake. Many Jews had already been crucified by the Romans, and every crucifixion led to more oppression. The Jewish leaders had no choice but to turn over one man to the Romans to avoid putting the entire population at risk."

It was the most I had ever heard Uri talk, and at the moment I was more impressed with him than I was with Richard. He was calm and sure of himself. Richard's face was going blotchy, and I could tell he was having trouble maintaining the smile.

"Certain priests had to turn Jesus over to the Romans," Uri went on. "But it was after a ROMAN indictment before a ROMAN official who imposed a ROMAN punishment for a crime against ROME, that Jesus was crucified, by ROMAN soldiers."

"Then that's the difference between us," Richard said. His voice sounded relieved, like somebody when they know the answer on Jeopardy. "Those of us who know Jesus is the Savior would die for Him, not play it safe."

Before I realized what was happening, my hand was sticking up in the air. Stevie looked at me as if I'd just arrived with a heart for the transplant.

"In the first place," I said, "Jesus' own disciples scattered like a bunch of rabbits the minute Jesus was in trouble. And in the second place, we're not here to talk about the differences between us. We're here to find common ground. From what Hadassah said, Jews AND Christians are supposed to love God—body, mind, and spirit—and love other people. ALL other people. Including people who don't agree with us."

For a moment, Richard stared at me as if he were witnessing MY resurrection from the dead. Then his smile wobbled back into place, and he said, "Okay, I lost that round." He turned to Hadassah and grinned at her, too. "But that doesn't mean I won't try to witness to you."

She didn't smile back.

Then somebody else got up and asked if the Jewish kids would tell some of their stories of living in Israel with the Palestinians so close by. They all looked at their fathers in the back, who nodded almost without moving. We were glued to our seats for another thirty minutes while Uri and the cousins—in fact, all of them except Nava—told about the dangers of such seemingly innocent places as bus stops and cafes, where suicide bombings took place. They spoke of the constant alerts that more such attacks were on the way, fifteen to forty threats a day. Their voices caught when they shared the deaths of some of their relatives and friends who worked in terrorist-fighting groups.

"The war against Palestinian terrorism," Uri said, "has become a fight for personal survival."

"Is that why you're in the U.S.?" Alex from our youth group asked him. If my jaw could have fallen open, it would have. Mr. I-don't-need-a-youth-group? Go figure.

I saw Hadassah's eyes flash. "I would rather be there fulfilling my obligation to my country," she said.

There was a silence that had the unmistakable sound of respect. I was being tugged by it in a way I could actually feel.

When Stevie started to announce that it was time to eat and do the fellowship thing, I hurried up and took the mike from her.

"If anyone wants to sign up to keep this understanding open," I said, "come see me and put your email address or your phone number on a list. Maybe we could have another forum, or if something comes up about prejudice or something, we can all sort of get together on it."

I wasn't a tenth as eloquent as Hadassah, and in fact I heard a few people imitating my teeth-together speech as they made a beeline for the cookies, but by the time I got a sheet set up, there were already people waiting to sign it. Celeste sat with me, which I was sure accounted for most of the male participation.

The first person to come up was Mr. Howitch.

"I'm about as proud as I know how to get," he said. "Where do I sign?"

"You rock, Mr. H.," Celeste said.

"I'm going to take that as a compliment." Mr. Howitch smiled at me. "I have to leave, but you just contact me if you need anything."

About the fifteenth person to come up was Richard.

"Hey, Celeste!" he said. "How's it going?"

"Fabulous," she said. The sarcasm was dripping like the Big Bad Wolf's chops. To me she whispered, "Watch yourself, Duffy."

Richard was looking sadly at my mouth.

"What happened?" he said.

"Broken jaw," I said. My heart was pounding.

"How'd you do it?"

"I didn't. Somebody else did it for me." I shrugged. "It's a long story."

Go away—go away—please go away. I was afraid I was either going to spew out something ugly, or burst into tears.

Richard shoved his hands in his pockets and tilted his head at me.

Why did you have to do that? I wanted to scream. It was one of the mannerisms that had attracted me to him in the first place. It was so— genuine.

"I didn't know your group was coming," I said instead.

"I didn't know it was your group that was doing this. I mean, I'm glad to see you, but I'm surprised."

"I guess you would be," I said. "Last time you saw me, I was about half clueless about the Lord."

He didn't deny it. Sometimes "genuine" isn't the easiest thing to take. But he did say, "Looks like you got more than a clue, girl. You're one of the people who set this up, aren't you?"

"Yeah," I said.

Celeste slung an arm around my shoulders. "It was her idea."

"We all worked on it," I said.

I felt a hand on my other shoulder, this one belonging to Pastor Ennis. "Well, ladies," he said. "I think we have the start of a youth group here."

He gave us each a pat and hurried back to the Dayan men.

"Ya'll are starting a youth group?" Richard said.

It was hard for me to miss the admiration in his eyes. It obviously escaped Celeste entirely.

"Y'know, it's not like Laura hasn't always loved the Lord," she said. "And now, you don't even know the half of it. She's like, our teacher. J.B.

and Trent and me didn't even go to church before we got to be friends with her." She surveyed him coolly. "Like I said, you don't even KNOW."

Richard looked a little baffled, and I almost felt sorry for him. By this time, Joy Beth, Trent, and Stevie were all on the scene, hovering like parents. But the one thing I'd forgotten about Richard was that he had enough confidence for about thirty-seven people. His face split into a grin.

"Okay," he said. "So—where do I sign?"

"You want to be on the list?" Celeste said.

"Yes," he said. "You got a pen?"

When he was gone, the FF's pounced on me.

"Why didn't you tell him you already had a boyfriend?" Celeste said.

"I DON'T—"

"Like that ever stopped YOU," Trent said to her.

"This is different. I wanted her to show him that she moved ON after he hurt her like he did."

"I don't know about the head games," Stevie said, "but something about that boy just bothered me. He's cute as he can be, but—maybe it was those questions he was asking."

Joy Beth looked at her soberly. "Gee—he was talking like a Christian."

"That's not what I mean!" Stevie tossed her hair back. "It wasn't WHAT he was asking. It was the WAY he was asking—like he was blaming Hadassah and them personally for Jesus' death or something."

"Yeah, that does kind of defeat the purpose of this whole thing."

We took a few seconds to stare at Trent. *Wow,* I thought, *maybe Trent was really starting to get it.*

"You okay, Duffy?" Celeste whispered to me when the FFs were out of earshot.

"I don't know," I said.

"You're not thinking about going back with him?"

"No," I said. But I WAS thinking that it was nice to be looked at that way again. It was really nice.

After the rest of the crowd had finally been shooed out by youth pastors, Hadassah and her brother and cousins looked reluctant to go. Once we'd gotten them talking, they didn't seem to want to stop, even after their fathers had left.

"I tell you what," Dad said, "I'll take the ladder home in Uri's Navigator and you can all stay until I get back. Then I'll take some of you home so Stevie doesn't have to ride all over the Beach carting people."

I knew that wasn't the reason, but at least Dad was being cool about it and not broadcasting the fact that he was still trying to "protect me" from something that obviously wasn't going to happen.

"You're the man, Mr. D." Celeste said.

He waved from the door.

We settled into a circle on the floor of the fellowship hall with the Dayans, and Mrs. Ennis came by with a tray.

"Leftovers, anyone?" she said.

"I told my mom nobody would eat the rabbit food!" I said.

"I will eat it," one of Hadassah's cousins said.

"He will eat everything," Uri said.

And then they laughed. They actually laughed. I felt like I was going to melt.

So we prayed, and it worked, I said to God. *That rocks.*

The thought had barely curled through my brain, when a sudden explosive roar shook the air.

"What the HECK was that?" Celeste said.

That was the last thing I heard before little Nava began to scream, "Hamas! Hamas!"

There was a moment of frozen terror before all of us were suddenly up and tearing for the door. Uri had to pick up Nava, who was flailing her arms and still screaming, "Hamas!" One of her fingernails nicked my arm, but I just covered it with my hand and kept running, my heart halfway up my throat.

"It came from the parking lot!" somebody else shouted.

It had. We saw it the minute we burst out the front door of the hall.

The Lincoln Navigator was in flames.

That was when I began to out-scream Nava—with "Dad! Daddy—NO!"

chaptereleven

"Duffy, wait!"

I could vaguely hear Celeste screaming at me from behind, mixed with the continued cries of "Hamas! Hamas!" None of it stopped me. Only Joy Beth's bulk, suddenly in front of me, kept me from jumping right into the flames after my father.

"I have to get him out!" I shouted at her. "I have to get my father out!"

"Over here!" someone else called.

It was Pastor Ennis, over to my left. I dodged Joy Beth and ran toward him. He was crouched on the ground, shielding something with his body. I caught a glimpse of Daddy's ankles.

Once again, Joy Beth planted herself in front of me, and this time somebody grabbed me from behind.

"Let me go!" I screamed at them. "That's my father!"

"He's alive, Laura!" Pastor Ennis said. "Somebody call 911!"

"I want to see him!" I said. With one massive jerk, I freed myself from Trent's arms, my own out in front of me, pushing at Joy Beth. She staggered aside, and I flung myself down beside Pastor Ennis.

My father lay on the pavement, his face perfectly still, as if he had just dropped off to sleep in his recliner. His legs were sprawled as if they, too, were relaxed. But on the rest of him, there was nothing that wasn't torn and bleeding.

"Daddy!" I screamed again.

"He's unconscious," Pastor Ennis said—"and thank God."

"Are you sure he's alive? Daddy?"

From afar I could already hear the sirens, and yet it had already been a lifetime since I'd knelt down and found him ripped apart.

"He's alive," the Pastor said. "I don't see how—but, Lord have mercy, he's alive."

The sirens wailed their way closer. Behind us, Nava was still screaming, "Hamas!" I looked back to see Hadassah with her arms around her, pressing her sister's face into her chest. Nava was beating her on the back with her fists and gasping for air.

"She needs help!" Stevie said.

"I must call my father!" Hadassah said.

A police car careened into the lot, its doors flying open.

"Officer!" Pastor Ennis shouted at him. "We need a second ambulance!"

The parking lot was already a horrible symphony of sirens. The fire engine turned its hoses on the Navigator. Three more police cars. An ambulance that spewed out two paramedics who moved me aside and bent over my father.

The second ambulance arrived right after Hadassah's father did. Not even he could calm Nava down. She was screaming again, and shuddering, and wheezing. Her father pinned her arms behind her back and held her, but she jerked her head so hard I was sure her spinal cord would snap.

Minutes later they wheeled her to the ambulance, oxygen mask on her face, arms tied to the sides of the gurney. She was still whipping her head around, still screaming "Hamas" through the mask.

I would have given anything if my father had made even a sound. As the paramedics gave him oxygen and started an IV and got into his face and shouted, "Mr. Duffy? Can you hear us, sir?" he didn't utter a whimper. I could only shiver as Stevie and Mrs. Ennis held me up.

"Where's Celeste?" I said.

"She went to tell your mom," Stevie said.

One of the paramedics stood up. "All right—let's move!"

I didn't even ask. I just climbed into the front seat of the ambulance.

"You sure you don't want to ride with me?" Pastor Ennis called to me.

I shook my head woodenly. I wasn't leaving my dad. It was my fault he was in that ambulance. I wasn't leaving him.

But at the hospital, they wouldn't let anybody go beyond the double doors with Daddy. Mom was hysterical, and after she checked me over from head to toe to make sure I wasn't hurt, she collapsed in Mrs. Ennis's arms. A nurse took the two of them and Pastor into another room.

"There's a more private waiting area you can all sit in," a nurse said to the rest of us.

I knew I couldn't sit, but I followed Celeste, Joy Beth, Trent and Stevie into a small paneled room with three over-stuffed love seats. Hadassah was already in there.

She was on her feet the second she saw me.

"How is he?" she said.

"He's still alive," Celeste said. "Mr. D.'s tough—he'll make it."

"We don't know that he will," I said.

"Laura, honey," Stevie said. "Why don't you sit down?"

"You want me to get you a Coke?" Trent said. "I'm gonna go get you a Coke."

He fled.

"I don't want a Coke," I said.

"Then just sit down," Stevie said. "You're scarin' me, Darlin'."

"I can't," I said.

It was true. I couldn't sit. I couldn't cry. I couldn't even think. It was as if everything that was happening was surreal, and all I could do was stand and watch it swirl around me.

Until Hadassah put her hands on my shoulders and forced me onto a seat.

"I have seen this," she said to the girls. "This is shock."

"What do we do?" Celeste said.

Hadassah put her face close to mine. "Listen to me, Laura."

I thought, oddly, that it was the first time she had ever said my name. It was beautiful, the way she pronounced it.

"It was a bomb. I know this. It did not function properly—thank God, or your father would be dead."

"He's not gonna die!" Celeste said.

Hadassah kept her eyes on me, no more than a few inches away. I didn't move.

"That bomb was meant for us," she said. "For my brother and my sister and my cousins and me. It was planted in our car—to kill US."

"NO!" Stevie said. "How could that be? No one at the forum would do that!"

"And nobody who WOULD do it even knew we were having the forum," Celeste said.

"Yes, they did."

They all looked at me, but I could still only stare straight ahead, at Hadassah.

"Wolf knew—the time and the place."

"Honey, how?" Stevie said. "She IS in shock—"

"Because I told him. I invited him to come." I looked up at my friends. "I guess he did."

The horror in their eyes was what finally wrenched the cries from me. "It's my fault! I killed my father—it's my fault!"

Hadassah put her arms around me and pulled me in, and I pounded my fists on her back, just as Nava had done, until I was too tired to hit anymore. Stevie peeled me away then, and held me almost in her lap. Celeste covered me up with a blanket.

"You didn't kill your daddy," Joy Beth said. "'Cause he ain't dead."

"And it is SO not your fault that somebody planted a bomb," Stevie said. "You invited that boy to our forum because you were trying to do the God-thing. You didn't say, 'Oh, and by the way, this would be a good time for you to blow up somebody's car!'"

Hadassah shook her head. "The truth of this matter is, there would have been no bomb if WE had not been there. This is about hatred for US."

"And for US for not hating you," Stevie said. "It doesn't compare to what happened to Mr. Duffy, but when I got to my car to come over here, all four of my tires had been slashed. We had to ride with the Ennises."

Joy Beth grunted confirmation.

Hadassah suddenly put her head in her hands.

"It's not your fault either," Stevie said.

"No," she said into her palms. "But if you were not involved with us, these things would not happen to you. That is why I did not want to be your friend." She stood up. "Take this as a sign and let us fight our battles on our own, for your own safety. I came here to say good-bye."

"No!" Celeste said. "What about YOUR safety? They didn't get who they wanted tonight. What if they try again?"

Stevie squeezed me tighter. "Cel-e-este—hel-lo!"

"Sorry," Celeste said. "Come on, Hadassah, sit down. This isn't over."

"How is Nava?" Stevie said.

Hadassah perched on the edge of the couch. "They have sedated her. My father is with her."

"What's that thing she kept screaming?" Celeste said. "That 'Hamas'?"

"It's that Palestinian radical group," I said. The strangest things were coming out of me. I sank back into Stevie's lap.

Hadassah nodded. "Nava is terrified of them. They set fire to our home in Israel."

"I'm no psychiatrist," Stevie said, "but it looked to me like she relived that whole experience when she saw your car on fire."

"We don't have any Hamas here, " I said.

"All we got's Rednecks."

I looked at Joy Beth. She was moving toward the door.

"Where are you going?" I said. My mind struggled for a clear spot.

"To find me some," she said.

"No—Joy Beth!" Stevie said.

But Joy Beth opened the door.

"You don't even have a car," Stevie said. "What are you going to do, RUN after them?"

"If I have to."

"I'll drive you," Celeste said. She fumbled in her bag for her keys.

"You guys—no!" I said. I pushed the blanket off and struggled to sit up.

"This is dangerous!" Hadassah said. "You have seen what they can do!"

But Joy Beth had already disappeared into the hall. Celeste turned to us, hands around her mouth, and whispered hoarsely, "I'll try to talk her out of it."

I could already hear Trent doing that very thing, outside the door. Moments later, all three voices faded away.

"She didn't look like she was going to be talked out of anything," Stevie said.

I wriggled from her arms and looked at Hadassah. "It would help if they found those guys and turned them in," I said.

"If they are not shot in the process!" Hadassah shook her dark head. Even her velveteen eyebrows looked weary. "I did not think they would go this far, these anti-Semites," she said. "There have been rocks thrown through our windows. Eggs smashed against our house. Firecrackers in the mail box. But nothing as serious as this bomb."

"You didn't tell us about all that!" I said.

"What could you do? The police did very little. They said they were looking for these 'vandals,' as they called them, but they did not look very hard."

"Vandals, my eye!" Stevie said. "They're terrorists!"

"Yes, we know that now, do we not?" Hadassah gave us both a sad smile. "You have been very kind, but it is time that you protect yourselves—"

She didn't get to finish the sentence. Mom opened the door and stood there, face ashen.

"Mama?" I said. "Is he—"

"They've taken him up to surgery," she said. "He'll be in there for several hours."

"Do they think –"

"I don't KNOW!" Mom pinched the bridge of her nose between her fingers and closed her eyes. "I'm sorry. They gave me something to calm me down, and it's making me jumpy."

I went to her with my arms out. She sagged against me like an old dog.

"I want you to go get some sleep," she said. "But I don't want you home alone. Go home with Celeste—"

"She can come to my house!" Stevie said quickly. "Celeste already left."

"Where's Bonnie?" I said.

"With Mrs. Ennis. I hope she'll be safe there. How do we know if any of us are safe anywhere? The church parking lot, for heaven's sake—"

Her voice broke and I tried to hug her, but she pulled away.

"Go sleep," she said. "I'll call you in the morning."

"Mom—I want to stay. This is my—"

"Just GO, Laura—please!"

She spread out her hands and then hurried out. I had a feeling it wasn't the medication that was making her jump down my throat.

"Your mother is right," Hadassah said. "Go and be safe."

"No," I said. "I'm staying right here."

Stevie's cell phone rang, and she hurried out with it, away from the accusing sign on the wall that said, PLEASE TURN OFF ALL CELL PHONES. She popped her head back in a moment later and said, "That was my father. He's coming to get me. Laura, please come with me."

"I'm not leaving my dad," I said.

She hugged me hard and left again, but not before I saw the tears in her eyes.

"You have good friends," Hadassah said. "That is a blessing."

"Yeah, but you're right about one thing," I said. "I bring a lot of trouble on them, just like I do my family."

"Why is that?"

Her eyebrows were knit together, as if she really wanted to know.

"Because I try to do what God tells me to," I said. "And half the time it drags me straight into some kind of impossible situation."

"And does it remain 'impossible'?"

I had to think about that before I shook my head.

"No, it doesn't. Nothing is impossible for God."

"When you pray."

"Right."

Hadassah shrugged. "Then why are we not praying now?"

I stared at her. "You mean, you and me?"

"Is there anyone else in this room?"

And so the Christian girl and the Jewish girl bowed their heads and the Christian girl prayed and the Jewish girl murmured in Hebrew. Sometime after that, I fell asleep with my head in Hadassah's lap.

chaptertwelve

When I woke up, there was a thin gray light filtering through the window, and Hadassah was gone. Mom was on the loveseat across from me, hair shoved into a curly knot on top of her head, eyes rimmed in red.

"Daddy?" I said.

"They just brought him out of surgery," she said. Her voice was brittle. "He's stable, but it's still serious."

"He's going to be okay, right? His face looked fine last night—and his feet—"

"Everything in between isn't fine. He's so torn up from being thrown across the parking lot, he hasn't come to yet. The doctor says the next twenty-four hours will decide."

I was afraid to ask just what they were going to decide. She looked dangerously on-the-edge, and I knew if I pushed her with anymore questions, she'd go right over.

"You need to go home and shower," she said. "Pastor Ennis is going to take you, and he'll stay with you when the police come to the house."

"Police!"

"They want to question you."

I was suddenly paralyzed. No matter how reassuring the girls had been the night before, they hadn't convinced me it wasn't my fault that

Wolf had known where the Dayans were going to be. Or that it wasn't my responsibility that we had the forum in the first place. Or that I wasn't to blame for dragging my father into it.

"He's waiting for you out front," Mom said.

"The cop?"

She closed her eyes, though her eyelids were so swollen they barely shut all the way. "No, Laura," she said. "Pastor Ennis."

I got to my feet and went slowly for the door. I wanted her to stop me and hug me and tell me she wasn't mad at me. She didn't. Her very stillness shouted, If it weren't for you, Laura, none of this would have happened.

When the policeman got to our house, I was showered and dressed and half-heartedly sucking up some Ensure through my big syringe. The officer, a guy with a shaved head who wasn't much older than I was, nodded toward my mouth.

"That didn't happen last night, did it?" he said.

I shook my head. Maybe if I made him think I couldn't talk, he wouldn't question me.

He didn't buy it. He asked me to basically tell him what I knew about the whole thing, which I did. When I was through he glanced at his note pad.

"So—Wolf Somebody, Quentin Somebody, and Joe Philip Morris. And they're pretty much trailer trash, in your opinion?"

"I didn't say that!"

"Didn't have to. Any idea where they might be at this point?"

"No, sir," I said. I didn't add that I knew three people who might by now, though there hadn't been a message from Celeste or Joy Beth or Trent when I'd gotten home. I wasn't sure that was a good sign.

"Do you know of anybody else with a beef against these Israeli kids?"

"No," I said. "But I know it was Wolf and those other guys. Everything points to them."

"Except the bomb itself. Way too sophisticated to have been put together by a bunch of punks."

I was about to jump off the couch at the dude. Pastor Ennis put his hand on my arm.

"If it were that sophisticated," he said to the officer, "why didn't the entire car blow up? From what I understand, Mr. Duffy is only alive because the thing evidently malfunctioned."

The officer leaned back in the chair and crossed one foot over the other knee, head cocked slightly to the side as if he were about to divulge information we civilians couldn't possibly be privy to. I seriously wanted to vomit.

"It wasn't the bomb itself. That thing should have vaporized the whole vehicle and anybody within a hundred feet of it."

I shuddered all the way down into the pit of my soul. Pastor Ennis put a protective arm around my shoulders.

"Do you mind?" he said to the officer.

"Sorry. Point is, that was a bomb meant for serious business. As soon as that key turned in the ignition, it should have—"

"We GET the point," Pastor said.

The officer snapped the button on his ball-point several times. "Unless they had help, my guess is these kids—" He pointed his chin at his notepad. "—didn't make that bomb. That thing was built by somebody that knew what they were doing. Since 9/11 we're all trained to recognize terrorist activity." He leaned forward again, pen poised over the notepad. "Do you know anybody who had anything against your father?"

"No! And nobody knew he was using the Dayans' car. He borrowed it at the last minute to take the ladder home."

"How about the people who own the car? The Israelis?"

I stiffened. Pastor Ennis's hand squeezed my shoulder.

"What about them?" I said.

"Did they have anything against your father?"

"They never even met him until last night!"

"How well do YOU know them?"

I could feel the hair standing up on the back of my neck. The officer ran his hand across his bare scalp. "Look, we just have to explore all the possibilities."

"Possibilities for what? They were the ones who were supposed to be blown up, not my father. Wolf and the rest of them have been threatening all the Dayan kids ever since they moved here—and they knew which car was theirs because they threw a bottle at it one night in front of Books-a-Million. I was there."

"There was no complaint registered that I know of."

"The manager wouldn't even call the police," I said. I narrowed my eyes. "He could have cared less. Just like a lot of people."

The officer stood up, stuffing his notepad into his pocket. "All right—look—I'll let you know if we need anything else from you."

Don't even think about it, I wanted to snarl at him.

When he was gone, Pastor stood behind the chair the cop had vacated and gave me a long look.

"I don't think he really thinks Hadassah and the others had anything to do with it," he said. "He was just doing his job."

I pulled my arms tight around myself. "You know what? I bet if the Dayans had all been hurt in that explosion instead of Dad, he wouldn't be so anxious to find out who did it. I bet he'd be calling it a suicide bombing—that's how much he knows."

Pastor clasped his hands together in that nervous way I'd seen him do at our first youth group meeting. That seemed like a thousand years ago now.

"What can I do for you?" he said.

"Nothing—no, pray."

"You can count on that. You don't want to come spend the day with Betsy? She'll pamper you." He grinned. "Bonnie's eating it up. Betsy could barely peel her away from the Belgian waffles to get her to school this morning."

I begged off and told him I was probably just going to sleep all day.

That was, of course, about the last thing I could do. What I did when he'd left was curl up like a wound spring in the corner of the family room couch and shake, inside and out.

I'm supposed to pray for my enemies, I thought.

I'd prayed for them, and exactly what good had it done? I'd led them right to the scene, and now my own father might die because of it. I looked over at Dad's recliner—and his computer—and the inevitable pair of pliers he was always leaving on the coffee table that drove my mother bonkers.

I wound up tighter against the back of the couch. *God—Please— please don't let him die. I'll do anything—*

I knew better than to try to bargain with God. But I'd tried everything else. Heck, I'd even prayed with a Jewish girl, which was probably like a minor miracle.

I uncoiled a little, as if I were being tugged loose from myself. It probably had been a miracle that Hadassah and I had prayed together, and both of us with so much—what had Mrs. Isaacsen called it that day? Passion? All I knew was that it had felt like a God-thing.

I wanted to feel that again. I closed my eyes and tried to think of the things that were right. The list wasn't long.

Dad was still alive.

And I'd sent the police after the Wolf Boys—if Joy Beth and Celeste didn't already have them packed in a freezer just waiting for the cops to arrive.

Of course, if my FFs got a hold of them, those guys really WERE going to need prayer—-

Suddenly, I couldn't just sit there. The silken rope, the one that had been motionless for so long, was pulling me toward the computer, where I logged on to AOL. Then I reached into my backpack. The Forum List was right where I'd put it last night.

I could smell smoke on it, the same burnt odor that had been on my clothes and was still on my backpack. It was an acrid smell I knew I was never going to forget, but it drove me on to enter all the names and email addresses into the Address Book and to pray for what I was going to say to them all.

I started off still not knowing, so I just explained what happened after they'd all left the church the night before, and I asked them to report any suspicious activity in the parking lot.

But the tug was strong to do more.

"What, God?" I whispered.

All I could think of was Mrs. Isaacsen telling me to respond in love. And Jesus, in those Bible verses, saying to "live out our God-created identities, the way our Father lives towards us."

Generously and graciously. Even when we're at our worst.

For a few minutes, all I could do was put my head down on the desk and sob—big, dry, painful choking things that strained the wires against my teeth and made them ache. I was at my worst, all right. I couldn't imagine being lower. All I wanted was to see somebody pay—but that felt so wrong, so un-Laura. So un-God. I couldn't stand another second of wanting to scream at police officers and snarl at kids who didn't get it and kick in the teeth of Redneck idiots. I was even sick of myself for thinking in labels that made me no better than they were.

I could no longer bear the sneer that my very soul was wearing.

My fingers were shaking so hard I could hardly get them to type, but somehow I managed a few more sentences on the email:

If you know anything, anything at all that might help the
cops catch whoever planted that bomb, please go to the police.
But do it out of concern for the Dayans. Whoever wanted them
out of the way isn't going to stop once they find out it didn't

work. Do it for the protection of our Israeli friends. Do it because it's right. But don't do it out of vengeance. Let's be the generation that stops the hate.

I sat back in the chair. Better. But I was still being pulled, and I wanted to be.

"What is it, God?" I said to the empty room. "What is it you want me to do?"

There was nothing. I got up and paced around, the anxiety pumping like barbed wire through my veins. I touched everything as if the answers were somehow in the furniture and the pillows and the pliers on the table. Only when I sank back onto the couch and stared at the blank television screen did I understand.

My reflected face was sneering back at me.

"Dear God," I said. "I'm ugly—I'm so ugly!"

I covered my face with my hands, but the picture of my own curled lip and my eyes pulled into slits was indelibly and starkly drawn in front of me. There was no getting away from it. And if I couldn't get away from that, what hope was there?

There is no hope if you try to do it on your own. There is every hope if you depend on Me.

Whether it was a whisper, a memory, or simply a revelation, I wasn't sure. All I knew was that it was the answer. If I were going to keep standing up against hate, then I couldn't have any of it in me. It had to start with me—and it had to start with each person who was going to read that email.

I scrambled back to the computer. My fingers were steady as I let what I hadn't known five minutes ago come out of them and onto the keys—as if I were taking dictation.

I'm making a pledge. It's my prayer for living from now on, and I'm asking you to pray it with me.

Father, make me a part of the solution.

Don't allow me to be a party to any kind of suspicion of people who are different from me. It tears them down, and they are your creations.

Help me to speak up when other people are showing their ignorance. Give me a heart that is sensitive to the hearts of others—even those who seem to have no hearts at all.

Strengthen me in my mission to set an example of a caring person and never, never let my lack of understanding hurt another human being.

I can't do it alone, God. Please empower my whole
generation to stop the hatred. And please remind us every hour
to pray for those who hate—for only then can we truly be like
your Son.

I could hardly see the screen anymore as I pressed the SEND button.

I was on and off the computer most of the day, although I really
didn't expect a reply from anyone until after school let out. I actually
hoped there would be something from Owen, but there was nothing, even
after I sent the same email to him. I at least expected a "You have
completely lost it now, girlfriend."

But it was quiet all day, and although I had my moments of near-
panic, every time I went back and whispered the prayer, I was calm again.
I had even dozed off in Dad's recliner for a few minutes when Mom came
in, everything on her looking scattered. Then I DID have an anxiety
attack.

"What's going on?" I said.

She dropped onto the couch and was about to lay her head against the
back when her eyes caught on the pliers on the coffee table. She picked
them up, held them against her chest, and burst into hard, rasping sobs.

"Mom?"

I leaped out of the chair and landed on the arm of the couch.
"Mom—is he gone?"

She shook her head. "He's regained consciousness, and he knew me,
and he can move. There's no brain damage." She held up the pliers. "He's
not out of the woods, but he'll probably be able to use these again, and if
he does I'm never going to complain. He can hang his tools on the walls
in here, and I won't say a word—"

Mom was laughing and spewing snot and hiccupping and pouring
out tears all in one operation. I wasn't doing much better.

"I'm so sorry this happened, Mom," I said. "I know it's my—"

"They didn't take him down. They thought they'd killed him, but
they couldn't do it."

I wasn't sure that my mother even knew what "they" she was talking
about, and I didn't ask. I just sat there with her until she conked out
against the arm of the sofa. When the phone rang, I dove for it before it
could wake her up. It was Stevie.

She was happy about the news about Dad, and she told me to have
faith that he was going to keep getting better. She also said she loved the
email. When I told her about Hadassah and me praying, she started to cry.

There was a lot of that going around.

"What did Celeste say?" I asked her. "I guess they didn't find the Wolf Boys or I would have heard by now."

There was a strange silence.

"Stevie?" I said.

"Celeste wasn't in school today, and neither were Joy Beth and Trent."

"No stinkin' way!"

"I called all their houses at lunch and acted like I was Blockbuster Video asking for them—you know, like I had a movie on hold for them. Joy Beth's mom and Trent's mother said they were in school. Celeste's father didn't answer—but there was no message like, 'Celeste, if this is you, get your tail home.'"

"He would have called here if he didn't know where she was," I said, "so they must have all gone home last night and skipped out today." A sick feeling was stirring in the pit of my stomach.

"Or else they told their parents they were going to spend the night at somebody else's house last night and just took off." Stevie blew her nose and then added. "I used to do things like that."

"This can't be good," I said.

"I'm sure they're all right—"

I took the phone into the kitchen and whispered into it. "Stevie, my father is in ICU—Nava's in the psych ward—so, no, I'm not sure Celeste and Joy Beth and Trent are all right at all!"

"Okay—so what do we do?"

I leaned against the bulletin board on the kitchen wall, the push pins poking me in the back like little reminders. "We pray," I said, "and we look for them." I shook the head she couldn't see. "That's stupid. I don't think my mom is going to let me leave the house after what's happened."

"Leave that part to me. I'll look by phone."

"Are you grounded?"

"Let's just say I'm in protective custody," Stevie said. "My father is a lawyer, remember? He doesn't trust anybody."

When we hung up, my hands were shaking again. I jumped when Mom padded into the room, squinting, hair standing on end.

"You okay?" I said.

"I'll make it. I'm going to take a shower and then we'll go back to the hospital. Dad wants to see you." That was all she said before she turned around and headed down the hall.

chapterthirteen

I sucked in air, and I don't think I let it out completely until I was standing beside Dad's bed in ICU.

"No more than ten minutes," the nurse whispered to me.

It seemed to take that long for Dad to open his eyes, and in the meantime I gazed at his face. It was unscarred—there wasn't a sign of injury except for the plastic tubes that hung from his nostrils. He looked almost peaceful. And thin. And old.

"Dad, I'm sorry," I whispered.

"For what?" he whispered back.

I gripped the rails on the side of the bed.

"I didn't know you were awake."

"I'm in and out." He made a weak attempt at a smile. His lips only went up on one side.

"Your face looks perfect," I said.

"Well, just don't look under the sheets. The rest of me isn't so perfect, they tell me."

My eyes blurred. "I'm so sorry, Daddy."

"Baby Girl, this is not your fault—and I don't have the energy to argue about it so don't start with me."

He tried the smile again, less successfully this time. I realized that after three sentences he was already worn out.

"The police will get them," he said. His voice was faint. "Stay safe."

He closed his eyes, but his brow was puckered. The tiny lines around his eyes had multiplied ten times since the day before.

"Don't hate them, Laura," he said. "You're too beautiful for that."

His breathing slowed. In a surge of panic I looked at the video screen with its green numbers and blips as if I knew what any of it meant.

"Dad?" I said. "Dad!"

The nurse poked her head in and her eyes, too, went to the screen.

"He's just sleeping," she said. She winked at me. "We have him on some pretty good drugs. We should all be so relaxed, huh?"

I nodded through my tears and retreated to the waiting room. Bonnie was there in Mom's lap, and Mrs. Ennis was opening a Tupperware container full of brownies.

"Bonnie and I made these for you," she said.

"Laurie can't have any 'cause of her wires," Bonnie said. She slid out of Mom's lap and wrapped her arms around my legs.

"It won't be long now, though, will it, Laura?" Mrs. Ennis said.

"Oh!" Mom shook her head like she was trying to get her brains to fall into the right slots. "Your appointment is tomorrow morning, Laura. To get your wires off."

"Oh. Yeah," I said. All the times I'd wanted to rip those things right out of my mouth, and now whether I had them on or not didn't seem like it would change anything that was important.

"I'm gonna make you a big ol' sandwich to eat," Bonnie was saying. "Peanut butter and banana and marshmallows..."

"Yummy," Mrs. Ennis said. She gave me a wide-eyed look.

"That'll be great, Babyness," I said to Bonnie.

Mom was looking at me. There was no forgiveness yet, but there was no anger either. Maybe she was too tired to feel much of anything, but I took what I could get.

"At least treat yourself to breakfast after your appointment," she said. "I don't care how late you get to school afterwards."

That, too, had none of the deliciousness it would have had twenty-four hours earlier. I closed my eyes and I prayed—and I prayed. And I prayed.

Please don't let me hate. Help me respond in love. Let my enemies bring out the best in me.

Mom and I went home not long after that, and I managed to get some sleep. She was already gone when I got up at 7:30, but there was a note reminding me of my 9:30 appointment and a twenty-dollar bill for buying myself breakfast afterwards.

Nothing sounded good to me, but I did open the trashcan lid and drop Big Bird's syringe unceremoniously into it.

"I'll celebrate when Dad and I are sitting here eating our cereal together," I said to the kitchen table.

The house was deadly quiet again. I hurried into the family room and logged on.

Still nothing from Owen. I swallowed down the lump in my throat. He was gone. I wasn't going to hear his voice again, and the loneliness opened up in me like a big empty hole.

But there were about twenty from people on the Forum List, and as I read, my heart seemed to physically lift in my chest. They'd written things like—

"I'm praying like no other."

"Let us know what we can do to help."

"My whole youth group is taking the pledge together tonight."

"Those Jewish kids are awesome."

"My mom wants to know if your family needs meals."

"I got there late," a kid with the screen name HOOPJOHN had written, "and I saw a guy in a white BMW sitting in the parking lot of the church. He looked like he was doing his homework or something. He was probably waiting for somebody that was at the forum—but you said to tell you anything suspicious. Somebody studying in a Beemer is WAY suspicious—but maybe that's just me..."

I wrote back to HOOPJOHN and told him to tell the police. The guy in the Beemer could have seen Wolf or one of them messing with the Navigator.

But it was the last email I came to on the screen that froze me to the chair.

It was from Richard.

"Hey Laura. Sorry to hear about your father. He's a cool guy. We're praying for him."

That much was okay, but something in the chopped way he had written it made me uneasy about reading on. Richard and I had exchanged enough emails back-when for me to know he could be a lot more eloquent. This reminded me of the let's-just-be-friends letter he'd ended our relationship with. It had that "I want to say what I need to say and get it over with" feel to it.

But I went on anyway. I've about heard every bad thing there is by now, I told myself. I can respond in love.

"I think you're right that the bomb was meant for the Israeli kids and not your dad," he'd written. "Violence like that is always wrong. It's like murdering a doctor who does abortions."

I blinked. *Where was this going?*

"You're right about hate too. And I don't hate the Jews. But they hate Jesus because they think all their suffering is because of Him. The truth is, they suffer because they don't believe in Him. Don't get me wrong—I wouldn't blow up their car or yell stuff at them in the halls. And nobody deserves to be hurt. But I'm not like you. I don't want to hang out with them. I hang out with Christians—and not just people who go to church but REAL Christians. I know you've really changed a lot and I can tell you love the Lord, and I'd like us to see each other again—as friends at first and who knows after that. But I have to say—you might not realize that the more you open yourself up to other people's beliefs, the more that'll eat away at your own. Christ wants you focused on Him."

"I'm not saying what happened Wednesday night was right—"

"You know what?" I said out loud. "I don't care WHAT you're saying!"

I pounded on the delete key about twelve times, and I would have kept mashing until I cracked the plastic if the phone hadn't rung.

It was Mrs. Isaacsen.

"You all right, darlin'?" she said.

"Yes, ma'am." I tried to control my breathing. "I'm having my wires off today, but I'll be in school later."

"Congratulations!"

"Thanks."

There was a sad silence. "How's your dad?"

I filled her in.

"I guess this takes some of the joy out of getting your jaw unstuck, doesn't it?" Mrs. I. said.

"Yes, ma'am."

"So—Celeste and Joy Beth are going with you?"

"Where?"

"To the doctor?"

I didn't have time to make a save. Mrs. Isaacsen read my silence.

"That's the phone message Celeste left for me at school this morning," she said. "She told me she and Joy Beth were taking care of you, and that's why they weren't in school yesterday and why they weren't going to be in today either."

"Oh," I said.

"You didn't know anything about that, did you?"

I hung my head over the back of the desk chair. "They're out looking for the Rednecks," I said. "I mean, you know, Wolf and those guys."

"How long have they been gone?"

"Since right after the explosion. I told them not to!" My voice was winding up.

"All right, now, let's try to stay calm. Celeste didn't sound like she was under duress on my voice mail."

"But if they're really hunting down Wolf and them day and night, anything could happen! I just thought they were going to look around town and—I don't know what I thought!"

"Okay. Take some deep breaths."

I did.

When I was no longer chugging like a freight train, she went on in her everything-is-under-control voice. "First of all, thank you for telling me all this, Laura. I have to pursue it, you know that. I'll try to do it with a minimum of trouble for Trent and the girls, but if I feel I have to involve the administration and the SRO's—"

"I'll understand," I said. "I just don't want them getting hurt."

"Will you be okay alone at the doctor?"

"Sure," I said.

Which was actually a lie. It turned out to be the loneliest experience I'd had since my first day at 'Nama High, and that was saying something.

There was no mom there to promise me a banana split as Dr. McKinney came at me with the clippers.

There was no burst of freedom as he told me to slowly and carefully open my mouth, for the first time in six weeks.

There were no FF's in the waiting room with banners and balloons when I came out of the office.

I thought of going to the beach. Mom had said she didn't care how long it took me to get to school, and it could be such good quiet time. But the thought of going to the same place where Richard and I had held hands and laughed—the Richard whose heart was so closed-off—no, I didn't feel like it.

I didn't even feel like singing, the way I'd waited to for so long. Not even "Your love is deep—your love is high—"

In fact, I didn't so much as say a word out loud until I got to school and opened my locker. THEN I opened my mouth—and screamed. Because hanging on the hook inside was a swastika.

I stifled the scream with one hand and slammed my locker door with the other. The sound echoed through the hall as I threw my backpack over my shoulder and ran all the way to Mrs. Isaacsen's office.

I was heaving in air when I got there, to find her door closed and a PLEASE DO NOT DISTURB sign hanging on the doorknob. It was all I could do not to pound on it with both fists. Instead, I choked back the sob that was rising in my throat and threw myself back out into the hall. My head was screaming for God.

I need to talk to her. I can't take this—I need someone—

Mr. Howitch.

Of course.

He was on his prep period when I got to the chorus room. It was a good thing it was empty because I burst in there with my words already clawing over each other to get out—

"Mrs. Isaacsen's with somebody—but I have to tell her—I have to tell someone—"

Mr. Howitch came off of his stool and was beside me before I could spew out the next burst of unintelligible syllables.

"It's not over, Mr. H.! They're still after them—they hung a swastika in my locker—and I know they have Celeste and Joy Beth and Trent—I know they do! We have to find them—we have to protect Hadassah—"

"Whoa, whoa, Laura—slow down."

Actually I had no choice. My face was burning, the muscles screaming at me that for Pete's sake they'd been dormant for six weeks and suddenly I was stretching them like they were bungee cords. I put my hands up to my cheeks and found myself gasping.

"Yeah, you need to sit down. Come on—"

Mr. Howitch guided me to a chair and made me sit. He wouldn't let me talk until I was breathing like a person who wasn't hysterical. I clutched the seams of my jeans so I wouldn't launch off again as I told him what was happening.

He pulled hard on his nose. I knew better than to interrupt that, but I wanted to scream, What are we doing to DO?

"All right—I'm going to call down to Mrs. Isaacsen's office," he said, "and then I'm going to call Mr. Stennis and have him get the SROs to make sure the Dayans are all right. They're all in school today except Nava."

I nodded. My heart was slamming into my ribs.

"I want you to sit right here and get yourself calmed down. We're going to get this worked out."

He strode across the room to his office, and I watched through the window as he picked up the phone, his finger busy at his nose as he talked. I couldn't hear what he was saying, but from the way his eyes were piercing the wall, I was sure the people on the other end were listening. I got calm enough to go back to praying.

I opened my eyes when I felt Mr. H's hand on my arm as he slid into the chair next to mine.

"The SROs are checking on the Dayans. Mrs. Isaacsen is on her way down here. She was handling a 'crisis.' There were four very unhappy people this morning when we posted the OM list. I guess three of them stormed her office." He shook his head. "They don't know what problems are, do they?"

I shook my head.

"I know Hadassah and Uri and two of their cousins were all happy that they made it, but with Nava still in the hospital and all this going on, that takes a lot of the joy out of it."

"There's a lot of that going around," I said.

He gave me a sad smile. "I see you got your wires off. It's nice to hear the Laura-voice again."

"I guess," I said. "All I really want is for all this hate to stop. I'm trying to love—I'm really trying."

"And you do it so well," he said.

Mrs. Isaacsen swept in then, the lines in her face crinkled into one big wreath of concern. She came right to me and put her arms around me. I started to sag, started to give in to the sobs, but I pulled away and looked at both of them.

"That swastika was a warning, I know it was. Are you sure the S.R.O.s are going to protect Hadassah?"

"Done," Mrs. I. said. "Mr. Stennis has them on it."

"And what about Celeste and Joy Beth and Trent?"

"I've contacted their parents. They all got the same story, that they were staying with you while your father was in the hospital." She looked at Mr. H. "Whatever happened to 'Parents—do you know where your children are?'"

"Well, at least we know they went wherever they went of their own free will," Mr. Howitch said.

"But they're not going to be free if they find the Wolf Boys!" I said. "We know what they can do—I tried to tell them that when they took off. I was hoping Trent could talk them out of it."

"Personally I can see Joy Beth holding her own against all three of those scrawny little creatures," Mrs. Isaacsen said dryly.

"If they have guns?" I said. "If they have a bomb?"

"Wait a minute," Mr. H. said. He ran a finger back and forth under his nostrils. "When was the last time you went to your locker before this morning, Laura?"

"Wednesday afternoon—late."

"So the swastika was put there either yesterday or early this morning. If it was the terrible trio who put it there, they're still in the neighborhood." He leaned toward me a little. "I know you aren't going to like this, but if we ask the police to put out an APB, they'll have them—and Celeste and company—within a couple of hours, I bet."

I took in a ragged breath. "Whatever it takes," I said.

The door opened, and a large black man in an SRO uniform darkened the doorway. He was one of the new ones they'd brought in after the gun incident. I felt guilty every time I saw him doing surveillance from under his hooded brow, even though I hadn't so much as dropped a candy wrapper on the floor.

"We've got a watch on the Israelis," he said. "I want to have a look at this swastika."

"It's still in my locker," I said.

I felt sick as the four of us took the long walk from the music wing to the locker area. Mrs. Isaacsen put her arm around me. The smell of her Chantilly was somehow comforting, at least enough to allow me to get my lock open. We must have been a sight, the three adults squatting, craning their heads behind me to get a look inside my bottom locker. I almost screamed again. At first glance, I thought the swastika was gone.

But it had only been knocked to the floor of the locker, which was where I discovered the note, typed on a piece of printer paper.

"I must have missed this before," I said as I handed it to the SRO. While he and Mrs. I. and Mr. H. stood up and crowded around it, I slid another note that was lying beneath it—the one in a parchment envelope —into my chemistry book.

Mrs. Isaacsen was reading out loud. "You've seen what we're capable of. We've seen the influence you have. Get the Jews out of 'Nama Beach High, or there will be more of the same.'"

I sagged against the bank of lockers. Mrs. Isaacsen grabbed me and held me against her. The S.R.O. handed the letter to Mr. H. and reached into my locker to pick up the swastika. I could barely bring myself to look at it.

It was cut cleanly out of cardboard and painted black. Red paint dribbled down its edges as if it had been carefully crafted to look like blood. A chill went through me.

It was much more polished than the graffiti that had appeared on the school wall. And the note did not have the ring of the words I could still hear in my head: *I believe in God. And I believe anybody that don't, oughta be run outa town.*

"I'm going to need to keep these," the S.R.O. said.

"Sure," I said.

The bell rang, but I had no idea what period it was.

"Why don't you have lunch with me, Laura?" Mrs. I. said. "You want to join us, Mr. Howitch?"

"I'll be there in five," he said.

Mrs. Isaacsen slung her arm around my shoulders again and steered me through the crowd that was already accumulating in the halls.

"Will this be your first meal without your wires?" she said.

"Oh. Yeah. But I can only eat soft stuff."

She gave my shoulder a final squeeze outside her office door. "I'm going on a search for some mashed potatoes, then," she said. "Get your taste buds ready and I'll be right back."

When she'd closed the door behind her, I wasted no time pulling my chemistry book out of my backpack and retrieving the note from the S.A.

> You have wiped away the sneer
> And you are now fit to offer a washcloth to your neighbor
> But give him more than that
> Give away your life.

I read it again, and then again, and each time it said that and only that.

"Give away my life?" I whispered to it. "How do I do that?"

But even as I heard Mrs. Isaacsen and Mr. Howitch talking their way toward the door, and I tucked the note into the pocket of my jeans, I knew he'd show me.

He always had.

chapterfourteen

Mrs. Isaacsen had not only scared up two helpings of mashed potatoes from the hot lunch line in the cafeteria, but she said she had somebody going out for frozen yogurt for my dessert.

"We have to celebrate a little bit," she said.

"I'm not celebrating until I hear her sing again," Mr. H. said.

"Yeah," I said. But I really didn't feel like either eating or singing. My mind was teeming with thoughts all poking up their hands for attention.

"Talk to us, Laura," Mrs. I. said. "If you don't, you're going to explode."

"I just wish there was something I could DO," I said. "I mean, besides pray."

She nudged the plate of potatoes toward me and tapped it with the tines of the fork. "There is a great deal of power in praying for your enemies. For one thing, it's very difficult to hate the very people you're talking to God about."

"I don't feel that much hate now," I said.

Mr. H. was watching me. "No, I don't see hate. I see worry. Concern."

"That's what I feel! That's why I want to DO something. I feel like everything I've tried to do so far has only made things worse."

"We don't know all the end results yet," Mrs. I. said. "People may refuse your love and reject you and your beliefs completely, but they have no defense whatsoever against your prayers."

"Even if they don't even know I'm praying for them?"

"Yes." She lifted a forkful of potatoes. "Open up."

I obediently opened my mouth as far as it would go, which wasn't far, and let the mashed spuds in. It was deliciously familiar to have something thicker than pureed oatmeal on my tongue. I felt like it deserved another try. Mrs. I. handed me the fork.

"While you're praying," she said, "pray for the OM team—or should I say, the kids that didn't make it."

"Have you talked to Daniel?" Mr. H. said.

I could feel my eyes widening. "Daniel didn't make it?"

Mrs. Isaacsen shook her head. "He's a brilliant child, but OM is a team, and he is not a team player." She grinned at Mr. Howitch. "Don't you sometimes forget that Laura is a student? We probably shouldn't be discussing this in front of her."

"He is REALLY going to be hacked off at the Jewish kids now," I said. "The ones that made it."

"Interesting," Mr. H said. "Seeing how Daniel himself is Jewish."

"No stinkin' way!" I quickly wiped the residue of the last forkful of potatoes from my lips. It was obvious I was going to have to learn to eat all over again. "I didn't know he was Jewish."

"And I'm sure he'd like to keep it that way." Mr. Howitch ran his finger up and down the length of his nose. "I ran into him at Books-a-Million one night and I asked him if he was interested in coming to a youth meeting we were having at the synagogue." He gave us a wry grin. "Twenty minutes later he was still expounding on the evils of religion—quoting Marx and Nietzsche and trying to convince me that only the weak need gods."

"What atheist got to him?" Mrs. Isaacsen said.

"I don't think it's so much that," Mr. Howitch said, "as it is some kind of deep-seated anger. I think he has the idea that God did him wrong somewhere along the line, and he's not going to open himself up to that kind of hurt again." He chuckled. "Listen to me telling you—you're the counselor!"

"No, I think you're right. He's smart—he's wealthy—the child drives a BMW to school, for heaven sake—but none of that is satisfying to him. Which is why I feel no guilt about not including him in OM. That wasn't going to fill the hole he's digging."

"He drives a BMW?" I said.

"Eighty percent of the kids in this school drive better cars than I do," Mr. H. said.

HOOPJOHN's email danced before me. I opened my mouth to tell them about it, when the phone rang. When Mrs. Isaacsen heard the voice on the other end, a shadow crossed her face, and she looked at me.

"She's right here, Mrs. Duffy," she said. "I'll let you talk to her."

I snatched up the phone and pushed it tight against my ear. I barely noticed Mrs. I. and Mr. H. slipping out of the room.

"Mom?" I said. "What's wrong?"

"Your dad has developed an infection," she said. It sounded as if she were calling me from the other side of the ocean, her voice was that weak. "They have him on massive antibiotics, but they're not sure they can fight it. Bonnie is going to stay on with the Ennises, and I won't be coming home until this is cleared up, so you need to—"

"Mom!" Enough with the lodging arrangements. "He's going to be all right, isn't he? Tell me!"

"I'm telling you everything I know, Laura."

"I'm coming down there."

"He's in isolation. They won't even let me go in right now."

"But I could be with you—"

"Laura."

I stopped. Suddenly I didn't want her to go on, to say I was the last person she wanted with her.

"I'm fine," she said.

"No, Mom, you're not. Nobody's fine right now."

"All right, I'm not fine, but I want YOU to be fine, and being here isn't going to make that happen. I want you to be with your friends. I know how much they care about you, and you always seem to work things through together. I can't help you that way right now, Honey."

Her voice broke. I didn't have the heart to tell her that my "friends" were nowhere to be found.

"Okay, Mom," I said instead. "But promise me you'll call me if—when—"

"I'll keep you posted."

There was a silence that needed to be filled up with something neither one of us could seem to say. All I could think of was, "I'm praying so hard, Mom. I'd give up my life for Dad."

Her crying garbled her words. I wanted to believe she said "I love you," before she hung up.

Mrs. Isaacsen opened the door a crack. "You okay?" she said.

I shook my head and told her the news. She took both of my hands in hers. "Why don't you just go home, Darlin'? Mr. Howitch said he doesn't need you at rehearsal today. You're not going to be able to concentrate if you stay here."

"You eat the yogurt when it gets here," I said.

I wasn't sure I wanted to be alone, but she was right that it wasn't going to do me any good to stay at school. Besides—maybe Celeste had left me a message—and if I could get in touch with HOOPJOHN, maybe I could get more details on the BMW. Maybe it was nothing—yet what if Daniel HAD seen something?

But I couldn't leave without at least trying to find Stevie. She was probably chewing those beautifully manicured nails right down to the cuticles by now. I was headed for the courtyard when Hadassah rounded the corner coming from the direction of the outside doors.

I flung my arms around her, nearly knocking a container marked Baskin Robbins out of her hand.

"This is for you!" she said. "Mrs. Isaacsen ordered it."

"You went off campus by yourselves?" I said. "They're supposed to be watching you!"

"We did not go anywhere. It was delivered by the Student Resource Officer." She knit her brows almost comically. "He was the largest human being I have ever seen."

"Did he have a forehead that hoods down over his eyes?" I said.

She nodded.

I laughed, and then I started to cry.

"It is good to be able to open your mouth?" she said.

"I guess," I said. I pushed the tears aside with my index fingers. Hadassah handed me the yogurt.

"I must go to my class," she said. "Oh—I have a message for you."

I pressed the cold container against my cheek, which was throbbing like no other.

"When I was outside waiting, a boy—no, a young man—he came to me and said he was going to leave a note on your car, but could I give you the message instead."

"Was it Trent?" I said. Adrenalin was already kicking in.

"No—this man was on a motorcycle. But I have seen glimpses of him before—I think he was there the day Nava found the gun in her locker.

He was tall. Attractive. He wore his hair pulled back and tied—what do you call that?"

I clenched my fingers around the container. "A ponytail," I said.

"But this was a handsome one. It was not like the ones worn by those—"

"What was the message?" I said. My voice shook, just like the rest of me.

Hadassah's eyes peered into mine. "Do you know this person? Is this safe?"

"What did he say?"

"He said for you to meet him at the church parking lot when school is over today." Hadassah was shaking her head. "Are you certain this is safe, Laura?"

I took in a long breath. It was Ponytail Boy. Of course it was safe. Except—on a motorcycle? Had he been hanging around with the Wolf Boys? What was THAT about?

Hadassah was watching me closely, so I forced a smile. "I know it sounds strange," I said. "But it's okay. I'll be fine."

As the bell rang and Hadassah hurried off to class, she didn't look like she believed it for a second. I tossed the now-melting yogurt into the nearest trashcan and headed for the parking lot.

I'd already slid into the Mercedes and was about to put the key in the ignition before I noticed the towel on the passenger seat. It was pure white, almost iridescent. Even my mother, the Laundry Queen, didn't get linens that clean.

"What the Sam Hill?" I said.

I reached across, almost afraid to touch it, but just as afraid not to, as if I might miss something if I didn't run my fingers across it. It was warm from the sun, and it was soft, like Bonnie's skin used to be when she was a baby, like the velveteen of Hadassah's eyebrows. Like soft words that said, Now you are fit to offer a washcloth to your neighbor.

I gathered it up into my hands and pressed it against my face. The muscles melted. My thoughts eased themselves quiet. I sighed out a prayer: I'll give up my life if that's what it takes.

Then I tucked it around my neck—a fabulous look with my tie-dye top—and drove home. I didn't feel alone anymore.

And I was even less so when I walked in the kitchen door and the phone started ringing. I dove for it, the words, Is he okay? already on my lips.

A husky voice said, "Duffy! What's happening?"

"Celeste?" I said—though who ELSE did I know from Brooklyn? She sounded like she was at least that far away. "Where ARE you?"

"Dothan, Alabama," she said—as if she were reporting on her vacation itinerary. "Now there's a hot town—"

"What are you DOING there?"

"Trackin' Wolves, baby—and we found them. All three of them."

"Are you okay?"

"Of course I'm okay. These fools are about as dangerous as the three blind mice. They're holed up in this cheap motel and they don't even come out for food. They send the manager's kid down to the vending machines."

"What cheap motel?"

"The one we tracked them to, thanks to some information from Joy Beth's third cousin—who overheard them talking Wednesday morning." Celeste grunted. "J.B.'s got more relatives than the Kennedys. Plus, Wolf and them are driving that big ol' honkin' truck that you can't miss—"

"Celeste!"

"What?"

Her voice was innocent. I didn't know whether to hug her or smack her. Good thing she wasn't there so I couldn't do either one.

"The police have an APB out on ya'll! We thought you were being held hostage by those creeps or something!"

"Nah, they don't even know we're here yet. We're still trying to figure out what to do with them."

"Don't do ANYTHING with them! They tried to blow people up, Celeste!"

"That's just it." I could almost see her wrinkling her nose full of freckles. Two bits she was wearing a Sherlock Holmes hat and a trench coat. "They couldn't have planted that bomb, Duffy. They've been here, at this motel, since Wednesday at noon. The manager says they haven't left at all. Unless they have some serious remote control thing going on, they had nothing to do with it."

I slid down the kitchen wall until I was sitting on the floor. My legs refused to hold me any more.

"Duff?" she said. "You all right?"

"No," I said. "Because if they didn't do it, then whoever did do it is still here. And they're not going to leave it alone."

"What? What's the deal?"

"They left a swastika in my locker."

There was only a short stunned silence before Celeste spoke in a low, serious voice.

"Duffy, be careful. Just stay put until we get home. We're only a couple hours away, less if I drive."

"You'll probably get picked up by the cops the minute you cross the state line," I said.

"Tell somebody we're comin'." I could hear her swallowing. "Duffy—don't go anywhere—don't do anything—I'm serious."

"YOU are telling ME that?" I said.

"Yeah," she said, "I am. Hey—you got the wires off."

"Yeah—"

"Just stay home and eat, then."

"Sure," I said. And before she could make me promise, I hung up.

"Don't do anything," I muttered as I dialed the number for 'Nama High. "Right."

Mrs. Isaacsen didn't answer her phone so I left her a voice mail: Celeste and Joy Beth and Trent are on their way back from Dothan. They found Wolf and them. They've been up there since Wednesday noon. I'm going to meet a friend at the church. Please tell the police not to arrest Celeste.

I didn't feel comfortable leaving that just hanging out there in Voice Mail Land, but I didn't have time to do anything else. School would be over in about five minutes, and I had a rendezvous. I grabbed my purse, and ran to the car.

I was halfway to the church before I realized that I still had the towel around my neck. I decided to leave it there. I was sure Ponytail Boy wasn't into fashion.

The only things I did know about him were that he could show up and disappear like a shadow, and, now, that he drove a Harley. I would be SO glad to see it—

But that thought careened to a halt when I turned into the parking lot. It was empty, except for a white BMW in the far corner. And Ponytail Boy wasn't in it. I could tell even from where I stopped that the guy in the car was Daniel.

chapterfifteen

My first thought was, *How bizarre is that?* My second was, *Is this his hang-out? Why doesn't he go to Books-a-Million like everybody else?*
My third thought, which was, *Where the heck is Ponytail Boy, anyway?* was cut off in mid-formation when the BMW revved to life and Daniel drove toward me. I moved my car out of the driveway and into a parking space so he could get past, but he pulled in next to me and rolled down his window.

"I see you got my message," he said.

"What message?" I said.

"The one I left with Mr. Howitch to give you sixth period."

I bit back the reply—I wasn't IN sixth period. Daniel didn't give me a chance to say it anyway. He leaned over to his passenger side and pushed open the door.

"Get in," he said. "I'll take you for a ride."

I shook my head. "I'm meeting somebody else here—too." I glanced anxiously around the parking lot, but there wasn't a sign of another car. I halfway wished Pastor Ennis would suddenly show up. And where WAS Ponytail Boy?

I looked back to see Daniel still staring at me. He hadn't closed the door.

"You WANT to hear what I have to say."

I laughed—for no apparent reason. "I do?" I said.

"You do. Get in. We won't go anywhere. We'll just sit here."

My stomach tightened. "Why don't we both just sit on the grass until my friend gets here—"

"I know who planted the bomb," he said. "If you want to know, get in."

I didn't even hesitate. Before I knew what I was doing, I was sitting in the leather seat beside him.

"Then you were here that night," I said. "You saw who set the car bomb?"

"Oh, yeah," he said. Then he was silent. He kept his hands tight around the steering wheel and stared through the windshield. His face was pale except for the black stubble of whiskers scattered on the point of his chin and under his nose. A few pimples stood out in garish red against the pasty skin.

My rational mind told me to make a break for it right then. The part that had to know what he knew told me to shut the door and try to warm him up. I paid attention to that one.

"Somebody said you were out here doing your homework Wednesday night," I said. I smiled at him. "Do you do that often?"

"What, homework, or come here?"

"Both—I mean, at the same time."

Daniel glared at the stone church across the parking lot. "I never go near a church if I can help it."

"Or a synagogue either?"

The minute it was out of my mouth, I wanted to snatch it back. Daniel turned toward me a face so livid it backed me against the window. I knew I wasn't hiding the fear in my eyes.

"How did you know?" he said.

"Um—I don't know—I heard it someplace."

"Liar," he said. And then, to my relief, he shrugged and sank back into his seat. "Doesn't matter now."

"What doesn't?"

"That you know I'm Jewish. That anybody knows. Actually, I'm only Jewish by culture. I don't practice."

"You pretty much have it down, then, huh?"

I tossed off a laugh. His face remained stiff.

"Sorry," I said. "I was just kidding. This goes pretty deep, huh?"

"Yeah," he said. "It goes deep." He was spitting out the acidic words more than saying them. I expected them to take the color right out of the leather. "It goes deep when you grow up in a school where you're the only Jew Boy from K through twelve. Where every time you turn around, some kid's got your yarmulke and he's flushing it down the toilet."

"What's a yarmulke?" I said.

Daniel made a sour face. "It's a little beanie Jewish men wear on their heads to advertise that they're prime targets for every bigot that crosses their path. And in my experience, every bigot is also a bully. Double jeopardy."

"Is that why you don't wear one anymore?" I said. I knew it was a lame question, but I knew I had to keep him talking until we could get back around to the bomb. I hoped it would happen before he himself exploded.

"No. I don't wear one because it means absolutely nothing to me. None of it does. I figured that out the first time I learned about the Holocaust—when I was nine years old."

Daniel turned sideways in the seat to face me. His face was oozing sweat, and the spikes of dark hair were wilting onto his forehead. The hand he rested on the steering wheel was trembling. I tried not to tremble myself. There was something very frightening about this boy.

"It doesn't surprise me that you learned about the Holocaust that young," I said. "You're so smart."

"Smart enough to figure out that all those people died for nothing."

"It was definitely senseless. Hitler was a madman—"

"I'm not talking about Hitler. I'm talking about them clinging to an identity that got them all incinerated—an identity that's never gotten anybody anything but worthless suffering."

I closed my eyes for a second before I asked the next question. "Are you talking about their suffering—or yours?"

"Theirs—mine—any fool's who gives up his life for something that never gives him anything back."

"Then you must have suffered something worse than just some teasing in elementary school," I said. "I mean, I know that's bad, but we all get over it—"

He lurched toward me so suddenly, so sharply, I gasped and shrank back. He planted a hand on the back of my seat, above my head.

"You think you could get over it if a Jew-hater kicked you so hard in the groin with his soccer cleats that you were deformed? For life? So you can probably never have—" He stopped and made quotation marks with his fingers as he hurled out the last words. "a 'normal male/female relationship'?"

I put my hand over my mouth and felt my throat constrict.

"Yeah, pretty grisly, huh?"

"I'm so sorry," I said. I sounded like I was choking.

"We had to move out of Biloxi just to get away from the people," he said. "When we came here when I was a freshman, I made up my mind nobody was ever going to know that there was a drop of Jewish blood in my body. And no one would have, if those Israeli kids hadn't shown up." His face flinched. "They had me nailed the minute they saw me. But there was no way I was letting them expose me."

"Expose you," I said. "You mean, to the same kind of treatment they were getting?"

He didn't answer. He didn't have to.

"So—how does this tie in with the bombing?" I said.

"At first I thought they'd get sick of those militia wannabes harassing them and leave, so I just bided my time. But they were tougher than I expected. " He shrugged. "I guess they'd seen a lot worse. Anyway, when I saw they weren't budging, I told Wolf I'd help."

I put my hand up to my mouth again. This was going somewhere I was sure I didn't want to go.

"Unfortunately they're even stupider than they look, those three. I provided them with the assault weapon, I figured out the combination on little what's-her-name's locker and left the lock so they only had to turn it one notch and it came right open. They handled that okay—but then I told them exactly what to buy to simulate a 357 magnum firing, and they screwed it up. They might as well have used caps for the puny sound they came up with." Daniel looked at me as if I would completely understand. "I was ticked."

"I can only imagine," I said. My voice had turned to plastic. I think my brain had, too. All I could do was listen, unbelieving.

"It might have worked, though," Daniel said. "These people around here are so ignorant, they were buying it."

"But you yourself were telling everybody they were wrong! That day in English—"

"Only because you had already stuck your nose in it—you and your merry band of Jesus Freaks. And then OM happened."

Slowly, I shook my head. He ignored it.

"There was no way I was letting those Jews take up my space on the team," he said. "No way. I worked my butt off to get where I am, and I wasn't going to stand by and let Bleeding Heart Isaacsen cut me out—or Howitch. With the two of them doing the choosing, I knew—I KNEW—"

He pounded his fist on the steering wheel. I jolted in the seat and then hung on with both hands. Every bit of sense I had was screaming at me to get out of that car. But something else was holding me back.

"I didn't know what to do," he went on. "I had about fifteen different plans but I threw all of them out. And then you—" Daniel turned to me again, and this time he smiled. It looked like an ugly wound cutting across his face. "You gave me just the information I needed when Wolf told me you invited him to the forum." He made a clicking sound with his tongue as he shook his head. "You've really got the religion thing BAD. You're the worst case I ever saw."

"So you saw your chance to kill ten people?" I said. "You were going to take them all out over a slot on a high school Odyssey of the MIND team? You didn't even know they were going to make it instead of you yet! But you planned to kill them for THAT!"

"NO!"

The word burst from him like the bomb itself, and the air in the car shook with it. I grabbed for the door handle, but Daniel threw himself across me and snatched my hand back from it. He kept it balled into a fist in one of his palms and, grabbing the other one, did the same thing. I fought back the panic that clawed at my chest. Somehow, over it, I could hear a whisper. I didn't know what words it was saying. I only knew it let me breathe. It let me say, "Then what did happen, Daniel? I'm listening."

"I never meant to hurt anybody!"

"Okay—okay—so what DID you mean to do?"

He let my hands to down to my lap, but he kept his fingers around my wrists—not as if he wanted to hurt me—it was more that he didn't want to me to go before he had the chance to say it.

I fixed my voice at a whisper. "What?"

Daniel's Adam's apple went sharply up and down in his neck.

"Wolf told me that little one—the youngest Jew –"

"Nava."

"He told me Nava was a basket case—on the verge of losing it. So I thought if I scared her bad enough, the whole family would pick up and leave with her. I've seen the way they protect her—it's like she's the Ark of the Covenant or something."

"That's true," I said. I softened my voice some more. "Go on."

"I just wanted to blow up the car. I made the bomb so I could detonate it by remote. I waited until it sounded like the forum was starting in there, and then I held off a little longer in case somebody was late. And somebody was."

HOOPJOHN, I thought.

"Then I set it up and parked around the corner." He pointed with his chin. "You all went on for hours. You could have negotiated a Middle Eastern peace treaty in the time you were in there. And then all of a sudden, all these people came pouring out, and I had my finger on the button."

I felt his thumb pressing against my wrist. His eyes glinted as he stared across the parking lot. Sweat was gathering in tiny bubbles within the lines on his forehead.

"But the Jews didn't come out. I watched some guy slash the tires on Stevie Martinez's car." Daniel grunted. "Hypocrite. By then my hands were sweating so bad I had to put the remote down so I could dry off."

That I believed. They were oozing perspiration onto my wrists even as we spoke.

"The second I let go, I saw the light go on in the Navigator, and I panicked—" Daniel's fingers tightened "—and I pushed the button." He looked at me, his eyes wild. "Even when I was doing it, I saw that it wasn't one of them. He hadn't even gotten in the car—I never meant for ANYBODY to get in the car. I was going to blow it up when they were walking toward it, when there was nobody else around it. I just wanted to scare them—I just wanted to show them that their religion isn't going to do a thing for them—"

He was no longer making sense, and I think even he knew it. He let go of my wrists and covered his eyes with the heels of his hands and rocked back and forth, his wound of a mouth pulled into a gash as he uttered hard, dry sobs.

I should have wanted to hit him. A normal person, I knew, would at least be screaming at him if not spitting on him and scratching at his eyes and tearing at his clothes.

But the person I was at that moment could only feel pity. *How hurt must you have to be,* I thought, *to go to those extremes just to cover up who you are?*

I put my hands up to my face, and for the first time realized the white towel was still in place. I pulled it off and held it out to Daniel.

"Here," I said, "wipe your face."

He pulled his hands down and blinked, uncomprehending, at the towel.

"Let me," I said. I wrapped it around my hand and applied it, gingerly, to his forehead. I didn't know whether he was going to start crying again, or snatch the thing from me and—

Do what with it? I tried not to let the expression on my face change as a chilling thought hit me. *Why did he just tell me all that? He's got to know I'm going to go to the police.*

Daniel put his hand over the one that held the towel and stopped it. His eyes searched mine like a little lost boy's.

"I just wanted you to know," he said. "So you could tell the cops that Wolf and the other two didn't do it. I gave them the money to leave town until—Just make sure the cops know it was me."

"Why don't YOU tell them?" I said.

He went on as if he hadn't heard me. "They ought to be locked up for sure, but not for attempted murder. Just for being pathetic."

"But if I tell the police, it'll just be hearsay—"

"I've backed it up in the note."

"What note?"

He just looked at me. What he meant hit me full in the face.

"Daniel," I said. "You're not going to commit suicide?"

"I thought you'd be glad. I practically killed your father. He still might not make it, right?"

But it wasn't gladness that flooded over me. It was something else, something painful—as if I could feel what was tearing him apart.

"Don't do it," I said. "Come on, Daniel—you're still a kid. You can change your life—GOD can change your life—"

"Don't talk to me about God!"

"There isn't anything else TO talk about right now!" I slapped the towel around his neck from behind and drew his face close to mine with the ends. "We'll all pray for you. We'll make sure you get help. There are a lot of us. We're out to stop the hate in our generation. You're throwing your life away because of hate, and it doesn't have to be that way. Please don't do this."

He searched my face again, eyes still lost. And then he jerked away and threw off the towel.

"Get out," he said. "I have to drive."

I shook my head. "I'll drive with you. We can keep talking until you clear your head."

"Get out, please," he said.

But he didn't sound convincing. I shook my head again, and he fired up the engine and peeled out of the parking lot. I could smell the burning rubber we left behind.

We screamed down Fifth Street, dodging cars and running stop signs. As we careened almost on two wheels onto Cove Boulevard and headed toward the Bay, I fumbled for the seat belt.

But what if that was pointless? Did Daniel have a bomb in here, too? Was he planning to blow himself up with one of his own concoctions?

I can't think this way! I told myself. *I have to talk to him. I have to stop him.*

He made a sharp turn onto Cherry Street, and I was thrown against him. I still hadn't found the seat belt.

"I DON'T want you to kill yourself, Daniel," I said, right into his ear.

He shoved me back into my seat with his elbow. "What do you care? You should hate my guts!"

"I can't hate you."

"Why not?"

"Because it only makes me ugly. I don't want to be ugly."

Daniel gave a hard laugh. "So it's all about vanity."

"It's all about God."

"I told you not to—"

"I know what you told me!" I grabbed for the dashboard as Daniel lunged around a motorcycle and squealed straight at the wall that separated us from the drop into the Bay. "And I don't give a flip! I'm praying for you whether you like it or not—and there's nothing you can do about it."

"I don't want your prayers. I just want to die."

"I don't! Stop now before you kill both of us!"

"I told you to get out." He jammed his foot on the brake and sent the BMW into a spin. The wall was inches away. I screamed and clung to anything my hands landed on. When we lurched to a stop up on the sidewalk, I was holding onto the gearshift and the back of his shirt. "Please get out," he said. A sob escaped from his throat. "I really don't want to take you with me."

"Then I guess you're not going," I said.

He tried to pull away from the hand that was still clutching his shirt, but I held on.

"What are you going to do, give up your life for me?" he said.

I felt a tug. A silken tug.

"If that's what it takes," I said. "I'd rather die for love than live in hate." I let out a sob of my own. "But I really don't want to die, Daniel."

He looked helplessly at the windshield, and then his eyes seemed to catch on the rearview mirror. He swore.

"What?" I said.

"It's that dude. He's following me again."

"What dude?" I said. "Is it the police?"

I got up on my knees and peered through the back window. There was a Harley behind us. Astride it sat Ponytail Boy.

I reached for the door handle, but Daniel grabbed my arm. "You're not leaving me?" he said.

"He's following you because he can help you," I said. "I'm just going to bring him to you."

I turned again to open the door. My startled cry matched the one from Daniel's lips. Mrs. Isaacsen was looking at me through the window, and crowding in beside her were Hadassah and Stevie.

Daniel turned frantically to the other side, his hands already groping for the handle. Mr. Howitch appeared in the window, Uri at his side. I managed to find the button that lowered the glass.

"Come on out, son," Mr. Howitch said. "We're here to help you."

Daniel looked back at me, and his face crumpled. I put the towel around his neck again and pulled him against me. Together, we cried.

chapter**sixteen**

Once Mr. Howitch left to take Daniel to the police station and Mrs. Isaacsen went off in the other direction to notify Daniel's parents, I had zero time to dwell on where Ponytail Boy and his Harley Davidson had disappeared to, or what could have happened inside that BMW.

Stevie started to run me through a litany of the possibilities as she drove me back to the church to get my car, and then she stopped herself with a shake of the curls.

"Okay, I'm sorry," she said. "You did the God-thing, of course. I don't know what else I was expecting."

"How did you guys know where I was?"

"That was a God-thing, too. I was in Mrs. Isaacsen's office and Mr. Howitch came in and told us about the message he'd just picked up for you. He had Uri with him, so we all just came to the church in two cars, and ya'll were just pulling out of the parking lot." She pulled her hand through her hair. "The way Daniel was driving, we all knew you were in major trouble. I thought I was going to watch you go right over that wall and into the Bay."

"It was so scary," I said.

"Which is exactly why you will not be alone tonight. And I don't want to hear any arguing about it."

I wasn't about to argue. I barely had the energy to hold my head up. I wasn't sure how I was even going to drive my car.

Not a problem. When we arrived at the church, Celeste's old Mercedes was parked next to mine. Celeste, Joy Beth, and even Trent were sprawled out on the church lawn like they were on spring break.

They jumped up the minute we pulled in, and Celeste was hauling me out of Stevie's car before she even got it in PARK.

"You morons!" I said as we held each other.

"Oh, we're the morons," Trent said.

Joy Beth grunted. "You were in worse danger than we were."

"How did you know already?" I said.

"Pastor Ennis," Celeste said.

"I called him on my cell phone," Stevie said. "And by the way, I am SO buying you one. At least then you can call us when you get yourself kidnapped."

We all spent the evening at Stevie's, being waited on by her mother (who was basically just like my mom but with hipper clothes and a Nautilus workout figure).

About halfway through her homemade enchiladas and my friends' saga of their mission to Dothan, I pretty much fell asleep on a cloud.

But I was awake and anxious the minute the sun came up. I left a note for Stevie and drove straight to the hospital. I'd had enough of this thing with Mom. I had to get it worked out.

She was curled up, asleep, on a couch in the waiting area. I went to the cafeteria for coffee and two huge cinnamon buns and wafted them under her nose until she opened her eyes.

"Mom," I whispered, "I brought breakfast and news."

"Laura—your mouth—how does it feel?"

She reached up to touch my cheek, and I started to cry.

"They caught the guy who planted the bomb," I said. "Well—he turned himself in. We're all safe now, Mom."

She struggled to sit up and took the coffee I handed her.

"I wish that made everything okay," she said. "Daddy still has a fever. It's not good."

I couldn't look at her.

"Laura."

I shook my head, my eyes still closed.

"Laura—"

"I know I'm responsible for Dad getting hurt—but don't you see, Mom—I had to stand up for those kids. I had to try to help people understand—"

"Laura, honey—I do see. And so does your daddy."

I opened my eyes and stared at her tearfully.

"And you forgive me?" I said.

"Forgive you—for what? For being brave?" Mom put her coffee-free arm around my neck. "You passed both of us in that department months ago. We're just trying to catch up. Now come on—" She picked up a gooey bun. "I want to watch you eat this."

We sat in the waiting room most of the day, visiting with the steady stream of people who came by, including Stevie and Hadassah who came during their lunch hour.

"We've got everybody praying," Stevie told me.

"We need more," I said. I gave her my password and asked her to get on her computer and send another email to the people on the Forum List.

"Done," she said.

As often as they would let us, Mom and I took turns donning masks and gowns and gloves so we could sit beside Dad's bed for ten minutes at a time. He seemed to be groping his way in and out of disturbing dreams.

In the late afternoon, the hospital started to close in on me. When Pastor Ennis stopped in to see Mom, I asked her if she minded if I went out for a while, just to clear my head..

It was an exquisite spring day, one of the reasons people lived on the Panhandle, Mrs. Isaacsen had told me once. When I got to St. Andrew's I pulled off my sandals and set off around the point, feet splashing in the bluest water on earth, until all things human faded into the background. Then it was me and the jetties and the pure white sand that the gulf breeze formed into water-like ripples at my feet. It was me, the pelicans— and God. I talked to Him out loud—because I could.

"I won't hate You if you let my father die," I said. "But I'm begging You, please don't. We're just starting to get along, he and I. I'm actually beginning to know him as a real person—and he's a lot more amazing than I thought. I'd even take his place right now—I WOULD."

I stopped and hugged my arms around myself. My sandals, dangling by the straps from my fingers, slapped against my lower back.

"I almost gave it up for Daniel, and I don't even know him," I whispered. "I would do it for my dad in a heartbeat."

I walked on, heading up toward the sand dunes. The memory of discovering those dunes with Richard stabbed at me. I had really liked him. I probably still would if it weren't for the email that revealed his attitude about Jews.

And what about Owen? He seemed to have abandoned me completely. Maybe, I thought, I should swear off boys completely, like

Stevie seems to be doing. Or just keep a string of male friends on the line, the way Celeste used to do. As if I could.

None of that eased the yearning I felt, a longing that was making me restless, even out here in one of my favorite God-places.

"If you were just here so I could talk to you," I said.

I wasn't sure who I meant. Owen, to clear the air? Richard, to set him straight?

Neither one, I thought.

I slung my sandals over my shoulder again and started up the dune. A silhouette rose from the top, a figure against the sun that made me stop ankle deep in the sand.

That wasn't Owen. Richard?

No. This tall young man had a thick ponytail that sailed out behind him in the wind.

I couldn't move. I didn't even breathe until he was right in front of me, smiling down at me, looking into me with golden brown eyes.

"You're all right now," he said.

It wasn't a question. I had a feeling he never needed to ask me anything about myself. There was something peaceful about being known.

"You saved me again," I said. "And I don't even know your name."

He tilted his head to the side to look deeper into my face.

"I didn't save you. It's your faith that saves you. You gave away your life—and it's been given back—given back with blessing."

My knees gave way and I sank to the sand. Everything was too real, too sharp, too clear. I couldn't bear it.

"Now," he said, "you have learned how to love recklessly."

For a moment I watched him walk to the top of the dune, and then I started up on my knees. "Wait!" I said. "Are you him—are you my Secret Admirer?"

He turned and smiled at me, and I had to close my eyes. The love was too much.

When I opened them again, he wasn't there. I didn't have to climb to the top of the dune to know that he was gone.

For now.

There was a sunset already sizzling on the horizon, and I knew I needed to get back to the hospital before Mom started pacing the waiting room. She was doing amazingly well, and I didn't want to push it.

But there was no urgency, no anxious what-am-I-going-to-have-to-face-when-I-get-there needling at the back of my neck. Still, I was startled when I pulled into the hospital parking lot and saw all of the BFF's, and more, setting up what looked like some kind of camp on the lawn. Celeste ran toward me with candles in both hands. She was dressed in white with filmy sleeves that floated like wings from her arms as she flew to me.

"What's going on?" I said. "What's all this?"

"This is a prayer vigil, Duffy," she said. "We're gonna pray until your dad is infection-free and Nava can smile again." She pointed across the grass to where Hadassah and Uri were lighting tea lights low to the ground out of the breeze. Mr. Howitch was perched on a rock nearby.

"We got everybody here, Duffy," Celeste said as she looped her arm through mine. "I hope you're impressed."

She wafted a hand in a grand gesture that took in more than 150 faces, all lit by candles. Near the front walkway, three guitar players had their heads bent together, tuning; and Trent was testing a microphone.

"How did you do this?" I said.

"YOU did it. Hadassah and Stevie just sent out an email to everybody on the list you made up—and check THAT out—"

She pointed to a banner that two of Hadassah's cousins were unfurling at the entrance. My prayer pledge was printed on it in bold black letters.

"I guess it pays to have that cheerleader thing in your blood." Stevie was suddenly on my other side, laying a kiss on my cheek. "I can still make a banner that kicks tail."

"YOU kick tail," I said. "You ALL do."

From somewhere in the crowd that was gathering around me, I heard the signature grunt.

"GOD kicks tail," Joy Beth said.

The guitar players clustered around the mike, and their words lifted up, even above the glow of the candles everyone held above their heads. They were singing the Jami Smith song—about God's love being deep—and high—

"Hey, Duffy," Celeste said at my elbow. "Come over here." She pulled me through the crowd, until we were behind a sea of backs. "I gotta tell you something you aren't gonna believe."

"I don't know," I said. "I think I've heard just about everything."

"Not this."

"Hey, Laura D."

I could feel my eyes widening as K.J. emerged from behind Celeste.

"Wow," I said.

"Her bein' here isn't even the half of it," Celeste said. "We've been talkin' on the phone all afternoon, and this will blow you away.K.J. and I have, like, a ton of stuff in common."

"No stinkin' way!" Stevie said. She stepped up behind me and put her arms around me, her chin on my shoulder.

"Way," Celeste said. "She has a mother with an addiction—I have a mother with an addiction. I got taken from my mother—she might get taken away from hers. She has a control weenie for a father—I HAD one." She gave a sly smile. "Only, I've been able to train mine."

K.J. glanced over her shoulders. Chief O'Toole was at the edge of the sidewalk, arms folded. I'd never actually seen the man before, but I knew it was him. He stood just the way K.J. did when nothing was going to get in her way.

"Mine's untrainable," K.J. said. "It's impossible."

Celeste nudged me. "I've been trying to tell her nothin's impossible with God."

"Excuse me if I have a problem with ANY father," K.J. said. "Even if he's 'heavenly' or whatever." She raked a hand through her hair. "That judge is gonna give custody of me to my dad no matter what happens. He's one of the good ol' boys. There's a whole club of them—I'm serious. It's like this big fraternity where everybody gets together and burps and farts and lies. They'd do anything for each other."

"Sounds like us," Joy Beth said. "Only we don't lie."

"And I don't fart!" Stevie said. She looked horrified.

K.J. sighed. "The thing is, I've decided I want to live with my mom. She started rehab this week—the first time she's ever done that—and I went to see her. She promised me she's going to deal with her problem and be a real mom."

The tears in K.J.'s voice surprised me.

"The only way the judge isn't gonna put me with my dad instead of her, once she gets out, is if I tell him the Chief smacks me around."

"Then you should do that!" I said. "He's got no right to abuse you."

"That's what I told her," Celeste said.

K.J. shook her hair back. "That's easy for ya'll to say. I'm the one who has to get up the guts to do it—in court. In FRONT of my father."

I snuck a glance at the Chief again. He had a face like a stone wall. Mt. Rushmore showed more compassion.

"So we have to help her, Duffy."

I looked at Celeste. "Okay," I said. "We'll pray—"

"But would you come?" K.J. said. "You know, like, be there in court when I testify?"

Stevie put her face closer to K.J.'s, shimmering in the candlelight. "You want us there?" she said. "You really believe that having us in the room praying for you will help?"

"Look, I don't know what ya'll have." K.J. looked off beyond us, blinking her eyes. "I guess it's God—I don't know. I just know when ya'll do—whatever it is that you do—things change."

My eyes locked with hers. "Then we'll be there," I said. "You just say when and where."

Celeste flung her arms around several shoulders until we were in a huddle, candle flames threatening to singe our hair.

"Before you girls start a bonfire over here, may we borrow Laura?"

We broke apart to let Mr. Howitch take one arm and Mrs. Isaacsen the other.

"You're here, too?" I said to Mrs. I.

"Wouldn't miss it. I had a delivery to make."

She opened my hand and tucked something small into it. I didn't have to see the flash of silver to know what it was.

"Prayer is the key to the power of love," she whispered to me. "Don't ever stop."

Then she folded my fingers over the tiny key and turned to Mr. Howitch. "She's all yours. Take her away."

"Where are we going?" I said.

"We are going to the microphone," he said. "Because you, my dear, are going to sing."

"Now? In front of people? I haven't even croaked out a note in six weeks—"

"I don't think he cares about that."

Mr. Howitch pointed upward, and at first I thought he was talking about God. Until I looked up and saw a thin figure in the window of my father's room.

It was Dad, giving me a feeble wave. It was weak, but it was all I needed to see.

"Where's that microphone?" I said.

Trent put it in my hand, and with my head thrown back and my eyes on Daddy, I opened my mouth and I sang— because His love was deeper and higher and longer and wider than I could have imagined.

I sang it, and the crowd sang it with me—the generation that was going to stop the hate.